MAID FOR
MONTERO

MAID FOR MONTERO

BY
KIM LAWRENCE

First published in Great Britain 2013
by Mills & Boon, an imprint of Harlequin (UK) Limited.
Large Print edition 2013
Harlequin (UK) Limited, Eton House,
18-24 Paradise Road, Richmond, Surrey TW9 1SR

© Kim Lawrence 2013

ISBN: 978 0 263 23219 6

Harlequin (UK) policy is to use papers that are natural,
renewable and recyclable products and made from
wood grown in sustainable forests. The logging and
manufacturing process conform to the legal environmental
regulations of the country of origin.

Printed and bound in Great Britain
by CPI Antony Rowe, Chippenham, Wiltshire

CHAPTER ONE

SOME MEN IN Isandro's position would have whined about press intrusion. He didn't. He considered he had little to complain about in life, and he knew it was perfectly possible, even for someone whose financial empire drew the sort of global media attention that his did, to have a private life.

Of course, if his taste had run to falling out of nightclubs in the small hours or the routine attendance of film premieres with scantily clad models, it might have been more difficult, but neither pastime held any appeal for him.

He viewed security as a necessary evil, a side effect of success—like midges in the Highlands—but he was hardly a recluse who lived his life behind ten-feet-high walls.

If he had had a family to consider, possibly he might have seen potential danger lurking around every corner, but he didn't. He only had an ex-wife, with whom he exchanged Christmas cards these days rather than insults, and a father he had very little contact with. Given that he was confident in his ability to look after himself, Isandro was not alarmed when the electronic gates that guarded the entrance to his English estate—which did actually have ten-feet-high walls—did not swing open as he approached, for they were already open.

Slowing his car, he swept the area with narrow-eyed, irritated speculation. While he didn't automatically assume this suggested anything dark and sinister, it did suggest a carelessness that he did not expect from those who worked for him.

The groove between his dark, strongly defined brows and his level of irritation deepened as his glance lighted on a brightly coloured bunch of balloons attached to an overhanging branch that looked incongruous beside the discreetly tasteful sign that simply read 'Ravenwood House: Private'.

He had owned Ravenwood for three years, and

in that time on the admittedly rare occasions he had visited he had never found cause for complaint, which was nothing less than expected. He employed the best, be they corporate executives or gardening staff, paid them extremely well and expected them to earn their salary.

It was not a complicated formula but one that he found worked, and if it didn't… He was not a man renowned for patience or sentimentality in his professional or personal life. If those in his employ didn't perform to the high standards he expected and deliver the goods they did not remain in his employ.

He opened the window, reached out and caught hold of the string dangling from the balloons. As he tugged two popped on the branches and the rest rose into the air, embracing their freedom. Following their merry progress with his eyes, he frowned before he pulled his head back in. He was not ready to read anything significant into the open gates or the balloons, but there had been a recent staff change, and the housekeeper did play a pivotal role at Ravenwood.

The previous postholder had not only been efficient, but had combined excellent man-management skills with the ability to blend into the background. She had never been obtrusive.

Under her watch he could not imagine open gates, invisible security or balloons. It was always possible none was connected with the new housekeeper, and he kept an open mind on the subject, innocent until proved guilty. No one could say that he wasn't scrupulously fair, and he made allowances for human error.

What he couldn't live with was incompetence.

He was prepared at this point to believe that the new housekeeper was as perfect as his personal assistant, who had interviewed the candidates, had indicated. He trusted Tom's judgement, as the younger man had always shown it to be excellent and it had been his efforts and diplomacy that had gone a long way to soothing local ill will when Isandro had bought the hall.

Three years ago the local community had greeted the change of ownership of the local estate with deep suspicion bordering on hostility.

The family that had given the house and the village their name had contributed nothing tangible to the local economy in decades, and the previous owner spent more time falling out of nightclubs and entering rehab clinics than repairing the roof or earning money to do so—so the locals' blind loyalty to them seemed perverse to Isandro.

With Tom's help he had addressed the situation with his usual pragmatism. He did not wish to be best friends with his neighbours, but neither did he want the inconvenience of being at war with them. The initial stream of complaints had faded to a trickle and visits from officials with clipboards from conservation and heritage groups that had halted work on the house and grounds had lessened and eventually vanished. He made a point of employing only local artisans and firms on the restoration work and made a donation that had put a new roof on the leaking church.

He considered the situation resolved.

Of all the houses he owned, this was the one where Isandro felt as close to relaxed as he ever did. It was beautiful and he enjoyed beauty. He invited none but his closest friends, and even then rarely. He never drove through the gates without feeling he was shedding the pressures of work.

He anticipated the next few days of rare relaxation, his wide sensual mouth twitching into a half-smile as he drove slowly through the pillared entrance. A moment later he was reversing.

The balloons snagged in the branch could have been accidental; this was not. Bizarrely tucked in beside one classical pillar was an upturned packing case.

With a mixture of growing incredulity and irritation, Isandro read the handwritten sign propped on it that informed him the eggs were free range and cost one pound per half dozen. There was no sign of the eggs mentioned, just a jar that was stuffed with coins and several notes suggesting trade had been brisk—the area had an unusual level of honesty.

Long brown fingers beat out an aggravated tattoo on the steering wheel. He had driven halfway down the long horsechestnut-lined driveway and was trying to rediscover his mellow mood when the noise hit him—a mixture of music, laughter, dogs barking and loud voices.

'What now...?'

Angular jaw set, he swore and floored the accelerator. A moment later he hit the brake, bringing the vehicle to a screaming halt on the top of the rise that gave him the first view of the delightful Palladian mansion considered by those in the know to be an architectural gem set in a parkland setting complete with lake, folly and beautifully tended formal gardens.

The manicured west lawn, where on occasion he watched invited guests play a game of croquet—and where he had spent the journey from the airport picturing himself enjoying the silence and solitude, sipping some brandy and perhaps catching up on some reading after the month of intense negotiations—was barely visible beneath the massive marquee, several smaller satellite tents, makeshift stage, cluster of stalls and what appeared to be a small...yes, it was a funfair of sorts, he realised as he identified the giant teacups slowly spinning to the strains of an early

Tom Jones number, the volume so loud even at this distance to vibrate in his chest.

Staring in unwilling fascination at the surreal spectacle, he started like someone waking from a nightmare as a voice over the loudhailer system announced the winner of the best behaved pet competition to be Herb—a result that, judging from the volume of the cheers and clapping, was popular.

Isandro swore loudly and at length in several languages.

The person responsible for this outrage would not be around to regret this invasion and misuse of his trust for long. For that matter he might sack the bunch of them because while this might have been the brain child of one person—presumably the new housekeeper—the rest of his staff must have sat back and let it happen, including his highly paid so-called professional security team.

Great! So much for leaving stress behind. His resentment levels rose as he mentally said goodbye to his much-needed, greatly anticipated break... So what if after a couple of days he'd get bored with the inactivity and grow restless? The point was he wouldn't have the option of being bored now.

The feeling he had wandered into some sort of alternative universe intensified as a balloon that had presumably followed him up the drive floated past his head. It snagged on a branch and popped—the sound breaking Isandro free of his teeth-clenched scrutiny of the disaster scene.

His dark eyes as warm as ice chips, he reversed with a screech of rubber back to the intersection in the drive and took the secondary road that led directly to the stable block at the rear of the house, which seemed blessedly free of the insanity taking place elsewhere on his property.

Entering the house via the orangery, he snapped grapes from the vine that grew in coils across the roof as he went. He made his way to his study, not encountering a soul to demand an explanation of or vent his simmering anger on. When he reached the inner sanctum, however, he did discover someone: a small child he had never seen before, who was almost hidden by his desk as she spun around in his swivel chair.

The child saw him and grabbed the desk to slow herself, leaving a neat imprint of sticky finger marks on the antique wood. His lips twisted in a grimace of distaste. He had few friends with children and his exposure to them had been limited to brief appearances at baptisms bearing appropriate gifts. None had reached this child's age yet... Five? Six? he speculated, studying the grubby freckled face.

'Hello. Are you looking for the toilets?'

The question was so unexpected that for a moment Isandro did not respond.

'No, I am not.' Was it normal for a child to be this self-possessed? She definitely didn't seem even slightly fazed to see him.

'Oh.' Hands on his antique desk, she began to twist in the seat from side to side. 'The lady was but the other man was looking for Zoe. Are you looking for Zoe, too? I can do fifty spins and not be sick. I could probably do more if I wanted to.'

Glancing at the Aubusson carpet underfoot,

he cautiously caught the back of the chair before she could put her boast to the test. 'I'm sure you could.'

'You picked grapes.' The kid stared at the grapes he had carelessly plucked from the vine as he had walked through the orangery. 'You're not meant to do that,' she said, shaking her head. 'You'll be in big trouble, and maybe even go to jail.' The thought seemed to please her.

'Thanks for the warning. Want some?' She seemed so at home he almost began to wonder if the place had been invaded by squatters and nobody had seen fit to mention it to him!

'Can't. You're a stranger. And they're sour.'

'Georgie!'

Isandro's head lifted at the sound of the musical voice with just a hint of attractive huskiness.

'I'm in here!' The kid bellowed back into his right ear, making him wince.

A moment later a figure appeared in the doorway. The body that matched the voice was not a let-down—anything but! Tall, slim, dark-haired with the sort of figure that filled out the faded denim jeans she wore to perfection. His immediate impression was of sinuous supple grace and an earthy sexuality that hit him with the force of a hammer between the eyes. Though the main physical response to her appearance was somewhat lower than eye level.

Isandro's aggravation levels reduced by several notches as he studied this new arrival, who didn't just have a great body but a vivid, expressive face he found himself wanting to look at. Stare at.

She possessed the most extraordinary eyes— electric blue that tilted slightly at the corners— and a mouth that made any man looking at it think of how it would feel to taste those plush pink lips… Isandro exhaled and reined in his galloping imagination. He had a healthy libido but he prided himself on his ability to control it.

'Georgie, you shouldn't be in here. I've told you. Oh…!' Zoe stopped halfway through the open doorway of the study. Her blue eyes flew wide as she sucked in a tiny shocked breath, registering the presence of the tall figure who was towering over her niece.

The strange reluctance she felt to enter the room was strong, but not as strong as her protective instincts, so, with a cautious smile pasted in place, Zoe stepped forward.

There had been many occasions in her adult life when she had been accused of being too trusting, too inclined to assume the best of others, but since Zoe had acquired responsibility for her seven-year-old twin niece and nephew she had developed a new caution that bordered, she suspected, on paranoia, at least when it came to the safety of her youthful charges.

Under the pleasant smile, her newly awoken protective instincts were on full alert. She moved towards the man whom she had not seen outside. And she would have noticed him, because despite the casual clothes—expensive casual—he definitely wouldn't have blended in with the carefree and relaxed people milling around outside.

She doubted that face did relaxed or carefree.

Without taking her eyes off the incredibly handsome stranger any more than you'd take your eyes off a stray wolf—and the analogy was not inappropriate, as he had the entire lean, hungry look going on—she held out her hand to her niece.

'Come here, Georgina,' she said in a tone meant to convey a sense of urgency without overly alarming her niece. Not that the latter would be likely—Georgie was friendly to a fault and she had no sense of danger whatsoever. Real parents probably knew how to make their kids sensibly cautious without scaring them witless and giving them umpteen issues later in life…but Zoe wasn't a real parent and most of the time she felt like a pretty sorry substitute for not one but two brilliant parents.

She took a deep breath and fought her way clear of the oppressive weight of emotions that continued to hit her when she wasn't expecting it. There wasn't time to feel angry at fate or the drunk driver whose carelessness had taken away the twins' parents. There was barely time to comb her hair some days!

'I'm sorry. I hope Georgina wasn't bothering you.' It was more polite than 'what the hell are you doing in here?' but in her experience it was always better to try a smile before you brought out the big stick.

Though it would take a very big stick indeed or even a small army to make this intruder leave if he didn't take the hint, she thought, sliding a peek at him under her lashes and looking away quickly. The heat climbed into her smooth cheeks as she realised her scrutiny was being returned, though there was nothing remotely surreptitious or apologetic about the way his dark eyes were wandering over her.

She flicked her plait back in a businesslike manner over her shoulder and, raising a brief cool hand to her cheeks, she wished that her protective instincts were the only reason she could feel the heavy, frantic beat of her heart in every inch of her body.

She'd never come across a man who exuded such a raw, sheer maleness before and it was deeply weird, not in a pleasant way, to find her indiscriminate hormones reacting independently to the aura he projected. She pressed her hand protectively to her stomach, which was quivering the way it did when she found herself in any situation that involved high places and the possibility of falling.

Logic suggested he was no danger to Georgie, just another visitor to the Fun Day who'd got lost or was just plain nosy but…the fact that she was the person whose job it was to protect the twins from everything bad in the world meant that Zoe was taking no chances.

'Now, Georgie, please.'

With a show of reluctance and a big sigh the copper-headed little girl responded finally to the note of command and slid out of the chair. But Isandro wasn't watching. His eyes were trained on the sliver of pale, toned midriff that was on show. The tantalising flash of flesh vanished as the woman's hand closed over the child's. Drawing her in, she bent to speak, saying something to the kid that made her nod before running out of the door.

Isandro watched as the young woman straightened up, throwing the fat plait of glossy dark hair over her shoulder again, exposing the firm curve of her jaw and the long elegant line of her pale throat.

The recognition that his response to her had been primal, out of his control, produced a frown that faded as he put the situation in perspective. Just because he had experienced an unexpectedly strong physical response did not mean he couldn't control it… Since his failed marriage he had never been in any form of relationship that he couldn't walk away from, and he never would.

She straightened up. 'Sorry about that.'

Now the child was gone some of the tension seemed to have left her slender shoulders, though a degree of caution remained in the blue eyes that studied him now with an undisguised curiosity mingled with a critical quality he was not accustomed to seeing when a woman looked at him.

Isandro's smile held a hint of self mockery… If she had not been beautiful would he have chosen to be amused…?

His appreciation of beauty was not restricted to architecture. He put this woman somewhere in her early twenties, young enough at least to wear no make-up and look good. Her clear skin was flawless, pale tinged with the lightest of roses in her smooth, rounded cheeks. She was not just sexy, she was beautiful.

Not in the classical sense perhaps, and absolutely nothing like the sort of woman he normally found attractive. For starters he dated women who worked hard at and took pride in their appearance. This woman's grooming left a lot to be desired, but her oval face with wide-set, slanting blue eyes, delicate carved cheekbones and wide, full lips had an arresting quality that combined sexiness with a sense of vulnerability.

Vulnerability was another thing he avoided in women. Needy was just too time-consuming, and time was a precious commodity.

His response simply proved that sexual attraction was not an exact science. Her look was not even smart casual, more scruffy casual. Despite his unflattering assessment of her style he was conscious of a heaviness in his groin by the time his eyes had made the journey up the length of her lusciously long, denim-clad legs. Tall and slender but with feminine curves that the over-sized white shirt she wore did not hide, she really did have a delicious body—and she would scrub up well, he decided, picturing her in something silky and insubstantial, and then in nothing at all.

He found his mood mellowing some more. The day might not be a total washout after all. He found himself more attracted to her than he had to a woman in months… It was possible that part of the appeal was she was not his type, not a samey clone. That and the clear-eyed stare, plus the extraordinarily sexy mouth, and the fact he felt confident that he could slide his fingers into her hair and not come away with a handful of hair extensions. Now that had been a real mood killer!

What had the kid called her…?

Not Mum, and she wasn't wearing a ring, but that didn't mean anything, so he remained cautious.

There were enough complications in life without inviting them, so Isandro kept his love life simple. He didn't do long-term relationships and was upfront about it, and even so he had never had to work hard to get a woman into his bed.

Married women, single parents, women who wanted commitment were not conducive to simplicity, so he ruled them out. He had learnt from his mistakes, and an expensive divorce that had lost him both a wife and a best friend provided a steep learning curve. Quite frankly there was no point in inviting problems when there were any number of attractive unattached women who did not come with baggage.

He could fight for a prize when it was required, but it was not his style to fantasise over the unattainable. He had no problem walking away from temptation, however attractively packaged, so he was surprised to recognise that in this instance it was a struggle to adopt his normal take-it-or-leave-it attitude.

Now that her niece was safely away from strangers she should have been able to relax slightly, but Zoe discovered she wasn't.

Obviously she had registered the fact he was not ugly the moment she entered the room, but she hadn't noticed the ludicrously long eyelashes, the jet-black, deep set heavy-lidded eyes they framed, or the incredible sculpted structure of his patrician features. Each strong angle and plane of his face was perfect.

He was her idea of a fallen angel—fatally beautiful and seductively dangerous—supposing angels were six-five and wore designer black from head to toe.

He smiled. It was usually possible to tell when a woman felt a reciprocal tug of attraction, and in this case it definitely was… She either wasn't attempting to hide her reaction or she didn't know how, not that she was trying to flirt with him, which was actually refreshing. Even a perfect vintage could become pedestrian if a man drank it for breakfast, lunch and dinner; he enjoyed flirtation to a point, but once you knew the moves of the modern mating ritual it could on occasion become painfully predictable.

A sense of expectation buzzing through his veins, he bit into the grapes. They were sour, as predicted, but he smiled.

The flash of white teeth and the intensity of the stranger's hard dark eyes sent a shiver through Zoe's body unravelling like a silken ribbon of desire. It was a relief when she finally discovered a flaw, which should have made him less attractive but had quite the reverse effect. The imperfection was relatively minor—a scar, a thin white line that began to the right of one eye and traced the curve of one chiselled cheekbone.

Zoe swallowed and plucked at the neckline of her shirt as the palpable silence in the room stretched. Her tingling awareness of him was so strong that there was a delay for several seconds before her body responded to the desperate commands of her brain. She was close to applauding with sheer relief when she managed to gather up the shreds of her self-control and lower her gaze.

'I'm afraid you shouldn't be here, either.' She pitched her tone at friendly but firm, it came out as breathy. Nonetheless, she was happy—breathy was a big step up from open-mouthed drooling!

Isandro's gaze lifted from the logo plastered

across the T-shirt she was wearing—not that he had read a word of the inscription, but mingled in with the mental image of him peeling the shirt over her head an astonishing idea had occurred to him, making the pleasurable picture fuzz and fade.

Surely not… She couldn't be…could she?

Had Tom lost his mind?

If she was, he definitely had!

Or had his normally super-reliable assistant been thinking with a different part of his anatomy when he appointed this woman to the post of housekeeper?

No, she couldn't be, he decided, clinging to his mental image of the perfect housekeeper—a woman of a certain age with an immovable iron-grey helmet of hair and a brisk manner. He didn't expect the new housekeeper to possess all the attributes of her predecessor but this woman—girl!—couldn't be…?

'This part of the house isn't open to the public, actually,' she admitted, softening the gentle remonstrance with a smile.

Madre di Dios, she was! Tom actually had lost his mind.

'None of it is but people keep wandering...' She heard the sharp note of anxiety that had crept into her own voice and closed her mouth, shaking her head as she smiled brightly and concluded in her best 'fasten your seat belt' tone, 'So if you'd like to follow me...?'

The irony of being asked to leave his own study was not lost on Isandro, but instead of putting this person in her place he found himself considering the question.

Would he like to follow her...? Yes, up the sweeping staircase and into his bedroom, which was not possible as he didn't date employees. It was a no-exception rule. But he was about to sack her, which would make her not his employee...?

Maybe Tom had been having similar thoughts when he had decided this woman fulfilled the brief of experienced and efficient. Maybe she possessed both these qualities in the bedroom? Maybe his assistant already knew...?

The possibility that his assistant had given his

girlfriend a job she was patently unsuited to because of her skills in the bedroom sent a rush of
rage through Isandro.

Was he mad because Tom had broken the rules,
or mad that Tom had broken them before Isandro
had got the chance?

Responding to the voice in his head with a
heavy frown that drew his dark brows into a single disapproving line over the bridge of his nose,
Isandro gave a frustrated grunt of tension.

When the tall, unsmiling stranger with his
film-star looks and smoky eyes didn't react to
her invitation to leave, Zoe felt the panic she had
been struggling to keep at bay all day surface before she ruthlessly subdued it.

She could panic when this day was over, even
though right now it felt as if it never would be.

How could anything that had started so inno-
cently become this monster? she asked herself
despairingly.

The answer was quite simple: she'd lost the ability to say no… She'd agreed to so many things

she'd forgotten or more likely blocked half of them; by this point if the Red Arrows did a fly past she wouldn't have been surprised.

CHAPTER TWO

IT WAS A total nightmare. In the past five days, she had lied more—by omission, which amounted to the same thing—than she had done in her entire life!

It was that first lie that had kicked it off and started the snowball effect, but the snowball was now the size of an apartment block.

It had seemed so innocent and she had been so desperate to help when poor Chloe, her dead sister's best friend—Chloe who always put on a brave face—had broken down in tears after inviting Zoe to a coffee morning.

'Who am I kidding? A coffee morning!' She shook her head in teary disgust. 'Do you know how much Hannah's operation costs?'

Zoe shook her head, guessing that such groundbreaking medical care in the States did not come cheap.

'And that's without the cost of travel to America. And time's running out, Zoe, while I'm organising coffee mornings and treasure. Baking isn't going to get Hannah to that hospital—it'll take a miracle!' she sobbed. 'In three months' time the disease might have progressed too far and the treatment might not work… They might not even agree to try and she'll be stuck in a wheelchair for life!'

Her heart bleeding for the other woman, Zoe hugged her, feeling utterly helpless.

'This isn't you, Chloe. You're a fighter. You're tired, that's all.' And small wonder. God knew when she had had a break; she commuted almost daily for Hannah's hospital appointments. 'Everyone's behind you, so involve us! We all want to help.'

She shook her head, wishing she had more than platitudes to offer the other woman. Then it came—the inspired idea—and she didn't pause to think it through, just blurted it out.

'Have your coffee morning at the hall. You know what people are like—they'll come just to have a nosy. We could put up some trestle tables in the garden and I'm sure Mrs Whittaker would bake some of her scones.' She knew that the entire community were gagging to see the changes made by the enigmatic new owner of the hall almost as much as they were gagging to see the man himself!

'Really?' Chloe had taken the tissue Zoe offered and dried her eyes. 'Won't Mr Montero mind? I wouldn't want to get you in trouble. I know when we asked if we could use the cricket pavilion for the charity match we got the thumbs down, though he did provide a nice shiny new cup for the winners,' she conceded with a sniff.

Wasn't hindsight grand? Of course it was easy now to recognise that this had been the moment to admit she'd have to run it past him, but she hadn't and neither had she run it past him afterwards because she knew what the reply would be. Chloe had been right: her new employer did not want to continue any old traditions or start any new ones of his own. He wanted, as Tom had explained, to keep the village the other side of the ten-foot wall.

'Not that he's not a great guy,' the loyal assistant had assured Zoe when he saw her expression. 'He's just private and he doesn't like getting personally involved. He's very generous, does heaps of stuff you don't hear about, but any charitable donations he makes are through the Montero Trust.'

The Montero Trust was apparently involved itself in such diverse projects as adult literacy programmes and providing clean water to remote Third World villages. It seemed worthy, but a solution loaded with red tape, and Chloe needed help *now*; she didn't have time to be at the bottom of a pile of worthy causes.

'Let me worry about that.'

And she'd been worrying ever since, but her reward had been Chloe's smile. She thought about that smile every time she got a fresh attack of guilt, which was often.

What had Tom said at her interview? 'He'll expect you to work without supervision, show initiative.' She suspected that today might be classed as too much initiative, but it wasn't as if the man would ever know. And his standing in the local community had been massively raised without any effort on his part. It was a win/win… or lose/lose for her if he found out!

No matter how hard she tried to rationalise what she'd done, Zoe knew that she had overstepped her authority big time and, as she was still working her trial period, if her actions were discovered the 'inspiration' could well lose her her job!

Her job…which meant her home and a roof over the twins' heads.

Small wonder she'd not had a decent night's sleep for the past week. And that was even before it had all got horribly out of hand. For some reason, once she had started saying yes she couldn't stop! Everyone had been so enthusiastic and generous, contributing their time and talents, that it had seemed churlish to be the one dissenting voice. The tipping point was probably the bouncy castle. After that Zoe had stopped even trying!

The only thing she could do today was stay on top of things and make damned sure that the grounds were returned to pristine condition once the day was over. She had an army of volunteers lined up for the task.

But right now what she had to do was get rid of this man—not as easy as it sounded because he made no effort to move as she stood back to let him pass—then check nobody else had wandered into the house.

'If you were looking for the toilets, go past the tombola and the refreshment tent and follow your nose.' In his case the nose, narrow and aquiline, was just as impressive as the rest of him. As she made a conscious effort not to stare their glances connected, only briefly but long enough to make all her deep stomach muscles contract viciously.

Seriously shaken by the extent of her physical response to this man, she huffed out a tiny breath from between her clenched teeth to steady her nerves and focused on a point over his left shoulder.

'You can't miss it.'

He still didn't take the hint. Instead he set his broad shoulders against the panelled wall and looked around the room.

'You have a beautiful home.'

Zoe folded her arms, hugging tight to hide her involuntary shiver. He had the sexiest voice she had ever heard and the faint accent only added another fascinating layer to it.

'No, yes...I mean it isn't mine.' It crossed her mind that he was being sarcastic. 'As I'm sure you can tell,' she murmured, flashing him an ironic grimace before extending a trainer-clad foot and laughing.

His hooded stare made a slow sweeping survey from her extended foot to her face. 'I try not to judge by appearances,' he drawled.

Her eyes narrowed. 'That's not always easy.'

Like now it was hard not to judge this man by the faint sneer and the innate air of superiority he exuded. She supposed arrogance was natural for someone who looked in the mirror each morning and saw that face looking back...and his body, from what she could see, was not exactly going to give the owner any major insecurities! Her gaze moved down the lean, hard length of his long body. Not only did he look fit in every sense of the word, he was supremely elegant in an unstudied, casual sort of way.

Her smooth cheeks highlighted by a rose tinge, she brought her lashes down in a protective sweep. If there was a time to be caught mentally undressing a stranger, this was not it.

'Actually I just work here…' The sweep of her hand encompassed the elegant room with its warm panelled walls and antiques. 'It is beautiful, though, isn't it?' A cross between a museum and a very expensive interior designer's heaven, the place, in her view, lacked a lived-in-look. There were no discarded newspapers, open books or sweaters draped over the backs of chairs, no sign at all that anyone lived there—it was just too perfect.

But then essentially no one did live here. It amazed her that anyone could own such a beautiful place and barely spend any time here at all.

The staff had been more than happy to fill

her in on the many houses owned by their elusive boss, and the many cars and private jets... Isandro Montero obviously liked to buy things whether he needed them or not. Zoe had always suspected that people who needed status symbols were secretly insecure. Mind you, having a bank account that hovered constantly just above the red made a person feel insecure too. Zoe knew all about that sort of insecurity!

His mobile ebony brows lifted in response to the information. 'So the owner has allowed his home to be used for this...event?'

Zoe felt her cheeks heat.

'How generous and trusting.'

If he had been trying he couldn't have said anything that made her feel more terribly guilty. Her eyes fell. 'He's very community minded.'

If he could hear me now, she thought, swallowing a bubble of hysteria as she imagined the expression on the face of the billionaire who didn't want to rub shoulders with the locals.

Her blue eyes slid to the wall lined with valuable books. Did he spend his time here reading the first editions on the shelves or were they, like the cricket pavilion, just for show…part of the entire perfect English Country Home?

What was the point in restoring a cricket pavilion if you never intended to use it? What was the point in buying books you were never going to read?

'The house is out of bounds today.'

He did not comment on the information. He was staring with what seemed to her far too much interest at a painting on the wall.

She went pale as for the first time she realised how vulnerable the house was. If he could just walk in here, how easy it would have been for someone to wander in—still was, and…not just someone! Her blue eyes suspicious, she turned to look at the tall stranger who continued to stare at the painting. God, she had been so sidetracked by physical awareness of him that it hadn't even crossed her mind that his presence here might not be accidental!

'There is an excellent security system in place, and security guards.'

He heard the nervousness in her voice, saw the sudden alarmed dilation of her pupils and smiled slowly, without feeling any sympathy. Well might she be worried, he thought grimly. The odds were that some of his valuables were even now in the pockets of light-fingered visitors. His security team would be lucky to come out of this with jobs.

'So I couldn't just pick up…' He made a show of looking around the room, then reached out and picked up a gilt-framed miniature from its stand. It was one of a pair he had outbid a Russian oligarch for six months earlier. He did not begrudge the inflated price, as he liked the sense of continuity—the miniatures were coming back to where they had been painted. 'This?'

The casual action made her tummy muscles flip. When she had first arrived she had literally tiptoed around the place, seriously intimidated by the value of the treasures it housed and scared witless of damaging anything. Though she had relaxed a bit now, seeing this valuable item treated so casually was alarming.

She gave a nervous laugh and thought, Calm down—no genuine thief would be this obvious... would they?

'No, you couldn't...' She sucked in an alarmed breath and fought the impractical urge to rush forward and snatch it from him. She didn't have a hope in hell of taking anything away from six feet five inches of solid muscle. She looked at his chest and swallowed, her tummy giving a nervous quiver as she pressed a hand to her middle where butterflies continued to flutter wildly.

'Is it genuine?' he asked, holding the delicate gilt frame between his thumb and forefinger.

'A clever copy,' she lied, nervousness making her voice high pitched. 'All the valuable stuff is locked away in the bank.' I wish!

'So that's why you're not concerned about stray visitors putting a souvenir in their pocket and walking out.'

Zoe swallowed as she watched the miniature vanish into the pocket of his well-cut jeans, but was able to maintain an air of amused calm as she returned his wolfish grin with a shaky smile of bravado and shook her head. What did it say about her that even at a moment like this she had noticed how rather incredible his muscular thighs were?

'We're not actively encouraging it, but if anyone's tempted we have a very strong security presence.' She saw no need to explain that this presence was at the moment helping out with directing people in and out of the parking areas. She felt extra bad about that because she had pretty shamelessly taken advantage of the absence of the head of the security team to persuade his deputy to relax the rules. She had used every weapon, including moral blackmail and some mild but effective eyelash fluttering.

'So I would be stopped before I left the building…?'

Even though she positioned herself strategically in the doorway, Zoe was well aware that he would find her no obstacle to escape if he wanted. Though she was not sure he wanted to— he seemed just as happy taunting her as making good his escape.

Zoe placed her hands on her hips, lifted her chin to a don't-mess-with-me angle and resisted the temptation to return an 'over my dead body' response. He might decide to take it too literally. Instead she said calmly, 'Definitely not. I'll have to ask you to return the miniature. It's very valuable.'

'Yes, it was quite a find.' The blue eyes he held blinked and a small furrow appeared between her dark feathery brows. He experienced a stab of guilt. She was obviously scared stiff and he did not enjoy scaring women even if on this occasion she deserved it.

'Find?'

He tilted his head in acknowledgement of her bewildered echo. 'The lady here was considered a great beauty of the day, but she was trade—the daughter of a wealthy mill owner. The marriage caused quite a scandal when Percy there brought her home.' He glanced at the twin of the portrait he held still sitting in its stand. 'It turns out that old Percy started a trend in the family, though I'm afraid the other heiresses that subsequent male heirs married were not always so easy on the eye as Henrietta here.' He studied the painting, taking a moment's pleasure from the masterful brush strokes and eye for detail shown by the artist. 'He really caught her... Such a sensual mouth, don't you think? Personally I think this is better than the Reynolds on the staircase.'

His eyes were trained, not on the portrait in his hand as he spoke, but her own mouth. The effect of the dark-eyed stare was mesmerising. Zoe didn't respond, mainly because she could barely breathe past the hammering of her heart against her ribcage, let alone speculate on how he knew so much about the history of the house and family.

'Maybe they were in love?' Her voice sounded as though it were coming from a long way away.

He laughed. The throaty sound shivered across the surface of her skin, raising a rash of goose-bumps. 'A romantic.'

The amused mockery in his voice made Zoe prickle with antagonism. What was she doing discussing love with a possible art thief? Was he? He certainly seemed to know more than she did about the artwork in the house.

'Actually, no, I'm not.' Her chin lifted. 'But if I was I wouldn't be ashamed of it. Now, Mr... I have things I need to attend to. If I could ask you to—'

'Shame is a very personal thing,' he mused, cutting across her. 'I wonder if Percy was ashamed of his heiress? You call it love, but I call it symbiosis.'

She compressed her lips. 'I wasn't calling it anything. I was simply not discounting the possibility.'

He tilted his dark head in acknowledgement of her interruption. 'Well, there is no doubt that she had money and he had social position, the ability to guarantee her acceptance into society, though maybe looking at that mouth there might have been other factors involved?'

He levelled his obsidian gaze on Zoe.

'Do you not think she has a sensual mouth?'

Now there was a case of pot calling kettle,

she thought, dragging her gaze from the firm sculpted outline of his own mouth.

'I'm no expert on sensuality.'

'I'm sure you are being modest.' He arched a satiric brow and the speculation in his smoky stare sent a rush of embarrassed heat over her body. 'Well, I shall continue to think that our Henrietta was a woman of passions…and that perhaps Percy was a lucky man? We will, I suppose, never know. What we do know is that when there were no more rich social-climbing heiresses, the family sold off treasures and land until finally there was nothing left. There is a certain sense of continuity in seeing this pair back where they started.'

'That's very interesting but…' She stopped, the colour fading from her face. His manner, his accent, the fact he displayed no sign of discomfort being caught in the house… Of course he had acted as though he owned the place, because he did!

How could she have been so stupid? Because he wasn't what she had been expecting, of course—

if she'd walked into a room and found a short, balding man using expensive tailoring to hide an affluent middle-aged spread she would immediately have considered the possibility that she was looking at her employer.

She squeezed her eyes shut. Small wonder the stable girl who had shown the double-page spread to her in the society magazine had looked at her oddly when she'd responded to the Welsh girl's enthusiastic, 'Isn't he utterly unbelievably lush?' with a polite but surprised response that he wasn't really her type. He hadn't been the man in the photo handing out the cup at the polo tournament—he'd been the one receiving it!

She had left the stables that morning reflecting sadly on the number of people who saw a man's bank balance before anything else. If the stout, balding man handing over the cup to the Latin-looking polo captain had not had the odd billion in the bank pretty Nia wouldn't have looked twice, and there she was acting as if he were some sort of centrefold pin-up.

My God, he was the centrefold!

Struggling to accept the evidence of her own eyes and lose the invented image in her head, she watched the polo-playing captain put the portrait back in its place.

I just knew this job was too good to be true.

CHAPTER THREE

'My name is Zoe Grace.' She lifted her chin and clung to a shaky façade of calm. 'I'm your new housekeeper, Mr Montero. I'm sorry, we weren't expecting you,' she apologised stiffly.

'So I was looking for Zoe after all.' He met her confused blue stare before his glance fell to the hand extended to him and, ignoring it, he continued in the same conversational tone. 'I think you'll find you're my ex-housekeeper. You may have managed to con Tom…'

Zoe's shock at the calculated insult was followed swiftly by anger that she couldn't check. 'I didn't con anyone!'

'Then I can only assume you're sleeping with him because I can't think of any other reason why Tom would employ someone so stupendously unsuited to this or, as far as I can see, any other position of trust. And before you waste your time fluttering your eyelashes at me I have to tell you I'm not Tom. I enjoy a good body and—' he paused, his eyes making a cynical sweep of her face before he delivered a crushing assessment '—passably pretty face, but when it comes to staff I prefer to keep the lines firmly drawn. It cuts down on confusion and time-consuming, messy litigation.'

Zoe hated him before he was halfway through the scathing tirade.

Dismay widened her blue eyes. He was already turning away. In the grip of panic she surged after him, catching hold of his arm. 'You can't sack me!'

He arched a brow and looked down at her hand.

Zoe let it go, biting down on her full under lip as she backed away, shaking her head.

'I mean, you can, obviously you can, but don't…' She swallowed and bit her lip. Unable to meet his eyes, she lifted her chin, a note of sheer desperation creeping into her voice as she added huskily, 'Please.'

There were times when a person had to swallow her pride and this was one of those occasions.

Of course, if it had been just her she would have told him where to stuff his awful job. In fact if there had been just herself to consider she wouldn't be doing the job to begin with.

But there was more than herself to consider now.

Even if she could get some sort of job locally that would enable the twins to continue going to their school—they'd had enough disruption in their lives without being snatched away from everything that was familiar—Zoe couldn't have afforded the rent on a property within the catchment area. As for buying—she would have been laughed out of any bank.

The property prices were inflated in the village because of the number of affluent parents eager to move into the area due to the success of the local state school. Laura and Dan had frequently joked that they were sitting on a fortune, but their lovely little thatched cottage had been taken by her brother-in-law's creditors along with everything else they had.

Though his expression did not soften, Isandro did after a short pause turn and face her.

'I need this job, Mr Montero,' she said, wringing her white hands in anxiety at the prospect of being jobless and homeless.

His expression held no hint of sympathy as he read the earnest appeal in her blue eyes.

'Perhaps you should have thought of that before you turned my home into a circus. Unless this is all someone else's fault…?'

Zoe didn't even consider passing the buck. She lifted her chin and thought, You got yourself into this, Zoe, now get yourself out—crawl, grovel, whatever it takes. 'No, this was all me.'

'And you're not even sharing the profits of this little enterprise…?'

Anger made Zoe momentarily forget her determination to grovel. 'Are you calling me a…?' She lowered her gaze and added quietly, 'I'm not making money from this. Nobody is!'

He arched a sceptical brow. 'No…?'

'All the money goes to a good cause a—'

He lifted an imperative hand. 'Please spare me

the sob stories. I have heard them all before. And as for appealing to my community spirit, don't waste your breath. I don't have any.'

Or a heart, either, Zoe thought, trying to keep her growing sense of desperation and panic under control.

She bit her lip. 'I know I overstepped my authority but I didn't see how a coffee morning could do much harm.'

His ebony brows hit his hairline. 'A coffee morning?'

She flushed and lowered her gaze. 'I know, I know…things got out of hand. It's just they were so enthusiastic and—' she lifted her eyes in appeal to his '—it was such a good cause that it was hard to say no.'

A flash of irritation crossed his lean features. If this woman expected he would react to a combination of emotional blackmail and big blue eyes she was in for a disappointment. 'It is always a good cause,' he drawled carelessly.

Zoe had to bite her lip to stop herself reacting to his contempt.

She bowed her head. If he wanted humble, fine, she could do that… She had to do that. 'We weren't expecting you.'

'How inconsiderate of me to arrive unannounced.' The sarcasm brought a flush to her cheeks. 'I admit I'm curious—what part of your designated role as someone responsible for the smooth running of this establishment did you think you were providing when you decided to turn my home into a cheap sideshow?'

'I thought…well, actually…I've already said it did get a bit out of hand, but it's not as if you are ever here.'

'So this is a case of while the cat's away. You have a novel way of pleading your cause, Miss Grace.'

'I need this job.' It went against every instinct to beg but what choice did she have? Speaking her mind was a luxury she could no longer afford. 'I really need this job. If you give me a chance to prove myself you won't regret it.'

His lifted his magnificent shoulders in a shrug. 'Like I said, you should have thought about that.'

He studied her white face and felt an unexpected flicker of something he refused to recognise as sympathy as he could almost taste her desperation. 'Have you actually got any experience of being a housekeeper?'

She was too stressed to give anything but an honest answer. 'No.'

'I think it might be better if I do not enquire too far into the reason my assistant saw fit to offer you this job.'

'He knew I needed it.'

Her reply drew a hard, incredulous laugh from him. Actually, he had some sympathy for his assistant. If her performance at interview had been half as good as the one she was delivering now, he would not have been surprised if the man had offered her more than a job.

He would be having words with Tom.

'If when I take an inventory there are any valuables missing you will be hearing from me. Other than that I shall expect you to have vacated your flat by the morning.'

Zoe gave a wild little laugh. Short of falling

to her knees, which might give him a kick but
would obviously not change his mind, what was
she meant to do? She had no skills, nothing to
sell… The sheer hopelessness of her situation
rushed in on her like a black choking cloud.

Falling back on the charity of friends was her
only option, and that was only temporary.

She made one final attempt.

'Please, Mr Montero.'

His mouth thinned in distaste. 'Your tears are
very touching, but wasted on me.'

She looked at him with tear-filled eyes. There
was no longer anything to lose by telling him
what she really thought. 'You're a monster!'

He shrugged. Being considered a monster was
to his way of thinking infinitely preferable to
being a sucker.

Zoe lifted her chin and, head high, walked towards the door, feeling the honeysuckle-scented
breeze blowing through the open window stroke
her cheek as she walked past him.

She was so blinded by the tears she fought to

hold back that she almost collided with the vicar who was entering the room.

'Oops!' he said, placing both his hands on her shoulders to steady her. 'Zoe, dear, we were looking for you.' In the act of turning to include in this comment the woman who stood beside him with the child in a wheelchair he saw Isandro and paused, his good-natured face breaking into a beaming smile as he recognised him before surging forward.

'Mr Montero, I can't tell you how grateful we are…all of us.'

Isandro, who had met the man on one previous occasion, acknowledged the gushing gratitude with a tilt of his head. 'The work is finished on the new roof?'

'New roof? Oh, yes, that's marvellous but I am talking about today. This totally splendid turnout. It warms the heart to see the entire community pulling together.'

He didn't have a heart to warm, Zoe thought as she saw the hateful billionaire tip his dark head and hide his confusion behind an impassive mask of hauteur. Actually it wasn't a mask; it was probably just him. Cold, cruel, vindictive, positively hateful!

'Mr Montero, oh, thank you... Hannah, this is Mr Montero, darling. Come and say thank you.'

Startled to find himself being hugged by a tearful woman, Isandro stood rigid in the embrace, his arms stiff at his side. Oblivious to the recipient's discomfort, Chloe sobbed into his broad chest and told him he was marvellous.

Zoe took a small degree of comfort from the discomfort etched on the Spaniard's handsome face. She'd have preferred a job and a roof over her head but it was something.

When Hannah propelled her wheelchair over, her little face wreathed in smiles, and informed the startled billionaire that he could have a puppy from the next litter, his expression almost made her smile...though that might have been hysteria.

'Bella is the smartest dog, even though she was the runt, and everyone wanted her last puppies, though this time we think the father might be...

Well, that's all right, you've plenty of room here and you look like a dog person.'

At a loss for once in his life, the dog person swallowed and wondered if the entire community here were off their heads.

Chloe still bubbling, her face alight, stopped her daughter's chair before it hit the desk. 'You two made this happen…' She took Zoe's hand and then that of the man she considered benefactor and pressed them palm to palm before sealing them between her own.

Standing there with a frozen smile on her face, Zoe had to fight the urge to tear her hand free. The only comfort she found in the situation was that he had to be hating this as much as she was.

'We made the target, so you won't have to shave your head!'

Zoe, forgetting for a moment her own situation, smiled happily, without noticing the expression on the tall Spaniard's face as he watched her light up with pleasure.

'Oh, Chloe, that's marvellous! Is there enough for John to come with you?'

'Not quite,' the older woman conceded. 'But he wouldn't be able to take that much time off work anyway. And we'll have so much to tell Daddy when we come home, won't we, Hannah?' She released the two hands she held and ducked down to her daughter, leaving Zoe standing there with her fingers curled around the long brown fingers of Isandro Montero.

While Chloe was kissing her daughter, and the vicar was taking off his glasses to study one of the paintings on the wall, Zoe took the opportunity to wrench her hand free and sling a poisonous look up at his face.

'Oh, Zoe, you've worked so hard. How will we ever be able to thank you? And don't you worry—we'll be here bright and early to clear away.' She stretched up to kiss Zoe's cheek. 'I wanted you to know first. Now I think we should go and tell everyone else...Vicar?'

'Yes, indeed. Mr Montero, you have a very impressive art collection here...amazing...' He wrung the younger man's hand with enthusiasm before following Chloe from the room. Zoe, who had tacked on behind them, was stopped by the sound of her name.

'Miss Grace, if I could have a moment…?'

Half inclined to carry on walking but knowing if she did the likelihood would be that the story would come out, Zoe paused and turned back, promising Chloe she would catch up. She knew it was inevitable that her friend would feel in part responsible for her sacking, but she saw no need to cast a cloud over this happy moment for the family who had not had a lot to be happy about recently.

She held herself rigid as he walked past her and closed the door.

'So?'

She shrugged and matched his tone. 'What?'

'Would you like to tell me what that was all about?'

Now he wants to know. 'I was trying to explain.'

Isandro's jaw tightened. He was furious to have been put in the position of being treated like some sort of hero and not having a clue why, and his anger was aimed at the person he held responsible for it.

'Well, explain now.'

'The fund-raiser was for Hannah.'

'The child in the wheelchair?'

Zoe nodded. 'Hannah had surgery for a spinal tumour. It was successful, they got all the tumour, but the pressure on the spinal cord caused damage and she can't walk. The doctors can't do anything, but Chloe, her mum, found a hospital in Boston that might be able to help. The treatment is experimental but so far the results have been really good.'

'And all this today was for that cause?'

She nodded.

His dark brows drew together in a straight line above his hawkish nose. 'Why on earth did you not tell me this straight away?'

She stared at him, staggered he could ask the question with a straight face... Priceless—the man was incredible. 'Possibly because you didn't give me a chance?'

Before he could respond there was a tap on the door and Chloe poked her head into the room.

'I almost forgot—we're having a party tomorrow at our house. Please come, Mr Montero.'

'Isandro.'

'Isandro,' she said, smiling. 'I'm sure Zoe will drive you if you want a drink,' Zoe was mortified to hear her friend suggest warmly. 'Her being the teetotaller she is.'

Zoe tensed, dreading the man would respond with a crushing refusal to the invitation, but to her surprise he simply nodded and said, 'Most kind of you.'

'Great—we'll see you both at seven.'

The door closed. 'Don't worry, I'll make your excuses. I'm assuming that as you know I'm not some sort of con artist you'll allow me to work my notice. I'm not asking for myself, but the children—'

Frowning, he cut across her. 'They all seem to be under the impression that I gave the go-ahead for this...this...'

'Fund-raising Fun Day.'

'Fun?'

'It started out as a coffee morning and then it just…'

He produced the sarcastic smile that made her want to stick a pin in him.

She clenched her teeth. 'Got out of hand.'

'It would seem you have a problem saying no.' He looked at her mouth and imagined her saying yes to a lot of things…yes and please. 'Did it not occur to you to tell me what this was about?'

She lifted her chin in response to his daunting disapproval and countered, 'Did it not occur to you to tell me who you were?'

The retort drew a frown. 'You have placed me in an impossible situation,' he brooded darkly.

Logic told him his hands were tied.

Sack her now and he would go from being the hero of the hour to the villain in a breath, and while he did not care overly for his standing in the local community, what bothered him was the press getting a sniff and running with it.

With the Fitzgerald deal in the balance the timing was as bad as it could be and this was the sort of story that the tabloids loved. The wheelchair-bound child, the rich landowner... He could see the headlines now, closely followed by the deal he had spent the last six months pulling together going down the drain along with all the jobs it would bring.

As tempting as it was to let the dismissal stand—every instinct he had was telling him she was nothing but trouble—Isandro knew the more sensible alternative was letting her stay. He had no doubt whatever that he would not have long to wait before she provided him with ample legitimate reasons to dismiss her.

An image of the pale freckled face flashed into his head. 'The child could not be treated in this country?'

Zoe smiled—the day had done some good. 'No, the surgery is ground-breaking.'

'And shaving your head?' He directed a curious glance at her glossy head, the light shining from the window highlighting natural-looking glossy chestnut streaks in the rich brown. 'A joke?'

Zoe lifted a self-conscious hand and flicked

her plait over shoulder. 'Not really. Chloe has bad days sometimes and to make her laugh I said if the day didn't raise the money she needed I'd shave off my hair to raise more.'

'No!' The strength of his spontaneous rebuttal startled Isandro as much as it appeared to the owner of the hair.

She blinked, startled. 'Pardon?'

'It would not be appropriate for my housekeeper to go around with a shaved head.'

For a moment Zoe stared at him, her hope soaring despite the voice in her head that counselled caution. 'Housekeeper. Does that mean…?'

'I will be back tomorrow and I expect—' He broke off as a great roar went up from outside. 'I will expect things to be back to normal.'

'So you're not sacking me?' Zoe lowered her gaze, appalled to find her eyes filling with weak tears of relief.

'I will give you a trial period.' He gave her a month.

'You won't regret it.'

He probably would. 'The child…?' He touched

the back of the chair she had been spinning around in. 'The one with the ginger hair.'

'Auburn. That was Georgie…Georgina.'

'She is…?' he prompted impatiently. It was like getting blood out of a stone.

'My niece.' She beamed happily. He could look down his aristocratic nose at her as much as he liked—she was no longer homeless, jobless and virtually destitute.

'She is staying long?'

'She lives with me and her twin brother, Harry.' In her head she could hear Laura on the phone when the scan had revealed she was carrying twins… One of each, Zoe, how lucky are we?

In the act of opening a diary on his desk, he stopped, his hands flat on the desk as he lifted his head. 'You have two children living here? No, that is not acceptable. You will have to make other arrangements.'

Zoe stared at him, breathing deeply to distract herself from the rush of anger. 'Arrangements? What,' she asked, 'did you have in mind?'

His eyes narrowed at the edge of sarcasm in her voice. 'I know nothing about children.'

'Except that you have no room in your twenty-bedroom house for two small ones.'

'So you're suggesting you move into my home.' He arched a sardonic brow and watched her flush. 'Or perhaps you already have?' It struck him that this might not be so far from the truth—the child had looked very comfortable in his chair.

Zoe flushed and bit her lip. 'Of course not.'

'So you would agree that the accommodation that comes with the job is not suitable.'

'It's fine.' It was free and in the catchment area of the twins' school, which made it not just fine but incredible!

His dark eyes sealed to hers as in interrogation mode he ran a hand across his jaw, shadowed with a day's growth of stubble. 'Correct me if I'm wrong...'

Oh, sure, I bet that happens a lot, she thought, struggling to keep her placid, perfect house-keeper smile pasted in place. She could see him now surrounded by little yes men falling over themselves to tell him how wonderful he was.

'But I was under the impression that the house-keeper's apartment had one bedroom?'

'A very big bedroom, and it has a perfectly comfortable sofa bed in the living room.'

'You sleep on a sofa bed?'

He could not have looked more appalled had she just announced she dossed down on a park bench or in a shop doorway.

'The arrangement works very well.' She smiled brightly in the face of his undisguised scepti-cism. If he was looking for an excuse to give her the push, she wasn't going to give him any. 'I'm always up before the twins, and they are in bed before me.' It wasn't a room of her own that kept Zoe awake at night, it was balancing her budget.

'In other words it is a perfect arrangement.'

Zoe pretended not to recognise the dry sar-casm. 'Not perfect,' she conceded calmly. 'But a workable compromise.' Like he knew a lot about compromise, she thought, but, smothering the prickle of antagonism, she continued serenely,

'And if you're thinking that the twins have a negative impact on my work, actually the reverse is true.'

'Indeed?'

'Having a family and responsibilities makes me ultra-reliable.' And totally lacking in pride, suggested the scornful voice in her head.

'You mean you need this job so you'll bite back the insult hovering even now on the tip of your tongue.' His hooded dark eyes slid to the soft full outline of her quite spectacularly sexy lips.

The words hovering on the tip of Zoe's tongue involved telling him to stop staring at her mouth.

She found herself thinking with nostalgia of the days when her temporary cash shortages had been dealt with by not buying the pair of shoes she'd been drooling over, or cutting back on the number of coffees she bought in a week. Things were no longer so simple. She was still reeling over the cost of new school uniforms for the twins, who had both shot up the previous term.

'You are speaking as if this arrangement is permanent. I assumed the children were spending their holiday with you.'

And I could have let him continue assuming that—the man is here so rarely he wouldn't have known the difference—but no, I had to go open my big mouth.

'No. They are my sister's children.' She swallowed. She didn't discuss the details of the accident that had killed her sister and her husband or mention the underage drunk driver going the wrong way on the motorway who had been responsible for the simple fact that she was afraid if she did she would start shouting. 'She and her husband died. I'm the children's guardian.'

'I am sorry.'

She nodded, not trusting herself to speak.

According to the grief counsellor anger was normal… It would pass, she said. There might be a time when she would stop being angry, but six months after that terrible day Zoe could not imagine a time when she would come to terms with it, stop wanting to beat her bare fists against a brick wall at the sheer terrible waste.

'You are very young to have such responsibilities.'

'That's relative, isn't it?' Only last week Zoe had watched a programme that followed a week in the life of children who were the main carers for their disabled parents. It had made her feel ashamed—compared to them she had it easy.

'Surely there is someone more suitable who could take care of these children?' He scanned her up and down and shook his head.

'My sister was my only family and Dan didn't have any family. It's me or social services.' She'd do what it took to stop that happening. The children would enjoy the sort of childhood she'd had… It was far too short as it was.

Zoe closed her eyes, remembering Laura's face the day she met Dan, and swallowed, concentrating on the anger, not the pain, as the same old question followed—why? Why Laura of all people in the world? Why did it have to be her?

He eyed her beautiful face cynically. 'I am assuming that housekeeping was not a career choice for you.'

Zoe moistened her lips, trying to decide what the right answer to this question was. In the end she kept it simple and honest.

'I never really knew what I wanted to do with my life.'

There had never seemed any hurry to make up her mind. She liked to travel; she liked new experiences and meeting new people.

Well, now it was her turn to step up to the mark and, yes, she would beg and be tearfully grateful to this awful man. She would grovel if necessary, even if it killed her. She would do whatever it took to keep her family together.

She gave a quietly confident smile. 'But I never give any less than a hundred per cent, and I'll do whatever it takes to keep this job… Anything,' she added fiercely.

'Anything…?'

Something in the way he said it made her feel less secure, but she wouldn't back down—she couldn't. She nodded.

'Absolutely.'

Expression impassive, he brushed an invisible speck off his dark top with long brown fingers.

'"Anything" covers a lot of territory so if you're offering sexual favours I should tell you I normally get it for free.'

Zoe's hands curled into tight fists at her sides as she breathed through the energising rush of anger. He was taunting her, but he knew full well she couldn't respond and in her book that made the man a bully. She rubbed the hand that tingled to slap the expression of amused disdain off his smug, impossibly handsome face, and tilted her chin to an enquiring angle.

But would she…?

She pushed away the question and willed herself not to blush, unwilling to give him the satisfaction of seeing her squirm. At least she was safe from any unwanted attentions—the man was obviously too much of a snob to consider sleeping with the help.

But if he did?

Her body reacted to the unspoken question and Zoe had no more chance of halting the visceral chain reaction than she did stopping her fingers jerking back from a hot object.

Taking a deep breath, she brought her lashes

down in a protective sweep and wrapped her arms across her middle in a hugging gesture, glad that she was wearing a loose-fitting top. She was saved the added embarrassment of having her shamefully engorged nipples on view, but it didn't stop her being painfully conscious of the chafing discomfort of her bra or the heavy liquid ache low in her pelvis.

Closing down this internal dialogue as her temperature rose, Zoe managed to break contact with his disturbing steely stare and lifted her shoulders in a tiny shrug.

'Jokes aside, I can promise you I shall be totally professional.'

He arched a brow and didn't look convinced by her claim. She felt panic trickle down her spine and thought, God, please don't let him change his mind.

'You won't be sorry.' Her fingernails gouged crescents into the soft flesh of her palms as she held her breath awaiting his response, feeling like a prisoner in the dock waiting to hear his sentence read out.

His tall figure framed in the doorway, Isandro turned. He already was regretting it.

'I am sorry for your loss, but I have to tell you I do not allow sentiment to sway my judgement, so do not expect any special favours here.'

Just how well would his judgement withstand the pressure of great legs and a stupendous mouth?

Her smile was cold and proud. 'I won't expect any.'

'We'll see. I judge by results, not promises.' Or lips, he thought as his gaze made an unscheduled traverse of the lush pink curve of her wide mouth before he could think better of it.

'I never had any complaints.' The unintentional innuendo after his previous comment brought a flush to her cheeks. 'In any of the jobs I've had,' she added hastily.

'That cannot be many. How old are you?'

'Twenty-two, and actually—' She lifted a hand, about to list the jobs she had done, and dropped it again, not wanting to give the impression that she didn't have staying power. As it happened, it was too late, as his next disturbingly perceptive remark revealed.

'What is the longest time you have remained in one job?'

Outwardly cool, inwardly thinking, Why, oh, why can I never keep my big mouth shut? she furrowed her smooth brow. 'Is that relevant?'

'It is if you walk after a week.'

'I have done a number of jobs, it's true, but who hasn't in this job market?' As if he knows such a lot about this job market. He may employ a lot of people in his various empires, but to him they are statistics on a chart. 'I've never left anyone in the lurch. I'm totally reliable.'

'But you don't like to stay in one place long? You have no staying power?'

'I have…' She forced her lips into a smile and bit back a retort even though it choked her to do so. 'Please don't judge me on first impressions. I have responsibilities now that I did not have previously.'

'We'll see.' He flicked his wrist and glanced at

his watch. 'My chef will be here later. You will make the arrangements.'

She nodded and produced a smile that oozed professional confidence. 'Of course.' She wrinkled her nose. 'What arrangements would they be?'

Unable to decide if she was joking, he regarded her with an expression of stern disapproval. 'This is not a work experience position, Miss Grace.'

'Of course not, Mr Monster...Montero.' Thrown into confusion by the horrifying Freudian slip, she almost fell over in her haste to get to the door before him to open it.

'I do not require grovelling. I require efficiency.'

She tipped her head meekly. 'Of course.' What he required, in her opinion, was taking down a peg or several hundred. She just hoped she was around to watch when it happened.

Passing through the door, Isandro revised his month estimate. She wouldn't last a week. If she had mouths to feed that was not his problem—he was not a charity.

CHAPTER FOUR

IF HE FOUND so much as a curtain fold out of place she'd eat her rather grubby trainers, Zoe decided, doing a final survey of the room.

The army of volunteers had cleared away any sign of yesterday's festivities in the grounds. The word had got around that the boss had put in an unexpected appearance the previous day and the staff had really gone the extra mile on the house. The rest of the rooms were equally pristine, about as lived-in as your average museum, but presumably cosy was not what he wanted.

Thinking the word 'cosy' in the same thought as Isandro Montero made her lips quirk, but not for long. She had spent a really awful night reliving yesterday's encounter, by turns breaking out in cold sweats when she thought of how close she'd come to losing the roof over their heads and seething with resentment that she'd had to crawl to keep it.

The couple of times she had managed to drift off she hadn't been able to escape the awful man who held their fate in his elegant, over-privileged hands. Shivering, she pushed her fingers into her hair and shook her head. Typical. She normally forgot the contents of her dreams the moment she woke up. But the dark erotic images from last night remained disturbingly fresh, as did the lingering shivery feeling in the pit of her stomach that did not diminish with each subsequent flashback.

Get a grip, Zoe, she told herself. The man only comes here once in a blue moon, so grit your teeth and give him no opportunity to criticise.

'You don't have to like him.' And you definitely don't have to dream about him, she added silently as she rubbed a suggestion of a smudge off the surface of a mirrored bureau door with the sleeve of her sweater.

Catching sight of herself, she gave a horrified

gasp. The house and grounds looked terrific but she didn't!

Rushing out into the square marble-floored hallway, dominated by the graceful curving staircase that rose to the second floor and the glass dome above that flooded the space with light, Zoe couldn't help glancing nervously at the big front door, her heart beating fast in reaction to the image in her head of it opening to reveal the master of the house. A shiver travelled the length of her spine before she shook her head, laughing.

Master?

'Really, Zoe!' She shook her head again, ignoring the fact her laugh this time had a breathless sound to it. Living with all this history was making her thoughts turn positively feudal, she decided, exiting through the door that led into a long winding inner hallway and in turn to the sturdy door that led outside into the quadrangle of outbuildings at the rear of the building.

She headed across the cobbled yard, past the rows of stone troughs filled with artistically arranged tumbling summer flowers, and up the stone steps that led to the flat above what had once been a coach house but now housed what was by all accounts an impressive collection of vintage sports cars.

Inside the flat she closed the door and leaned against it, relieved that he hadn't put in an appearance while she was looking like a scarecrow. Walking across to the fitted cupboard that housed her clothes, she grimaced at her reflection in the full-length mirror inside the door. Not exactly the image of cool efficiency she was determined to exemplify.

Stripping down to her bra and pants, she folded her jeans. When the space was limited neatness was essential but fortunately she didn't have many clothes, which made her choice of a suitable outfit pretty easy. Padding through the living room and through the twins' bedroom into the en-suite, she popped her dusty top in the linen basket, then pinned her hair up before she stepped into the shower. Though she would have liked to wash her hair, it took an age to dry and she was short of time.

Fifteen minutes later, wearing a crisp white blouse, a pair of narrow-legged tailored black trousers and with her hair in a fat plait down her back, she slid her feet into a pair of sensible black leather loafers. She gave herself a critical once-over, bending at the knee to see the top of her head in the angled mirror. Resisting the temptation to jazz up the sombre outfit with a pink scarf dotted with orange roses, she slid a pair of gold hoops into her ears. The sound of them jingling brought a smile to her lips as she lifted her head, more confidence in her stride as she headed across the courtyard. She was determined to make up for the disastrous first impression she had made; she could do it.

She had to do it.

Her smile faded slightly as she approached the building, tensing as she heard a car in the distance, but the vehicle that drove through the arch was a delivery van from the local butcher's. She started breathing again, delivering the silent advice, Cool it, Zoe, before she paused to thank one of the gardeners for donating a box full of the vegetables from the kitchen garden to the raffle the previous day, and admiring the magnificent lavender tumbling from a group of barrels.

'The smell always makes me think of summer and at night it fills the flat,' she told him, adding warmly, 'The flowers you cut for the house were marvellous.' She had spent a pleasant half-hour filling bowls in several of the rooms with the fragrant summer blooms.

He tilted his head in acknowledgement and looked pleased with the compliment. 'The other one here before you sent up to London for fancy arrangements every week. I told her it was a criminal waste.'

'I'm sure they were very beautiful.' The gardener might approve, but Zoe suddenly felt less secure about her amateur attempts to add a touch of colour to the house; they were hardly professional.

Resisting the impulse to run back to the house and remove all the flowers, which in her mind were fast becoming tasteless and ugly displays of amateurism, she chatted a little longer to the man before she finally excused herself.

In the end she couldn't bring herself to dump the freshly cut flowers, deciding as a compromise not to volunteer the information she was responsible—unless directly asked, which seemed unlikely. She walked around the place a final time to double-check everything, leaving it until the last possible moment before she jumped in her car and set off to pick up the twins from school.

For all she knew Isandro Montero might not arrive until midnight; he might be a total no-show—if she was very lucky.

The narrow country lane that led to the village was in theory a short cut, but Zoe got stuck behind a tractor, and the children were already waiting at the gate when she arrived, chatting to Chloe and Hannah.

'I'm sorry I'm late!' she exclaimed.

'You're not late,' Chloe soothed. 'They only just got out.' She took in Zoe's outfit and her brows lifted. 'Wow, you look very...'

'Weird,' supplied Georgie bluntly.

'Very sexy librarian,' Chloe corrected.

'Are librarians sexy?' Harry asked.

Chloe exchanged a look with Zoe, who suppressed a smile and said, 'In the car, you two.' Adding, 'Do you want a lift, Chloe?'

The older woman shook her head. 'No, I'm picking up some glasses for tonight from Sara on my way back.'

'I hope you all have a great night, I wish I could come but...' She lifted her slender shoulders in a regretful shrug; her babysitting arrangements had fallen through that morning.

'You can... I know, just call me fairy godmother. You know how John's mum is having Hannah? Well, she's offered to have your two as well. John will pick up the twins on his way home and he'll fetch them back in the morning.'

'Oh, Chloe, that's really kind but I couldn't impose...'

'It's not imposing. Maud offered and they'll have a great time, you know they will.'

'Yes, but—'

'Yes but nothing, Cinders, you're going to the ball and don't forget the invite includes your utterly gorgeous boss... I tell you, if I was a few years younger I'd give you a bit of competition there.'

Zoe struggled to smile at the joke. 'He's not here, I'm afraid.' She felt a guilty tug as her friend's face fell.

'I thought he was due back today. John's going to be so disappointed—he wanted to thank him personally and return his hospitality. Half the people there only came because they wanted to take a look at the hall.'

Zoe's unease increased. Short of admitting that the hospitality they wanted to return had not been given freely, she had no way of preventing the decision to treat the new lord of the manor as a community-minded philanthropist.

'He was...is...due today,' she admitted. 'But when I left he hadn't arrived.'

'But he might do.'

'Anything's possible,' Zoe admitted, but the thought of Isandro coming to a party where the glasses were borrowed and the food was provided by guests! Possible but not very likely, thank goodness!

'Well, promise you'll remind him if he does turn up? Tell him that we'd love to see him and he seemed very keen to come. He's obviously making an effort to be part of the community.'

Zoe didn't have the heart to shatter this illusion and explain that the man had only said yes to cut the scene short and get rid of them as quickly as possible.

'If he does I will,' Zoe promised, imagining with horror the admittedly unlikely scenario of Isandro putting in an appearance at the party. Him spending the entire evening with his lips curled contemptuously would suck the joy out of any occasion and Zoe wanted to save her friends that. On a less unselfish note she wanted to save herself from spending her precious off-duty time with a man who made her skin prickle with antagonism even before he opened his mouth and said something vile and unpleasant. The fact that half the vile things he said were actually the truth was neither here nor... Losing track of her train of thought, she shook her head slightly to banish the image of the lips that combined overt sensuality with an underlying hint of cruelty.

She was getting fixated on the man's mouth when it was the things that came out if it that she ought to worry about.

'John will be by around six to pick up the twins.'

Isandro did not get involved in other people's lives. His charitable donations to selected good causes were made anonymously, and he never responded to any form of moral blackmail or sentimental sob stories, but the story of the little girl and her 'last chance to walk' trip to America continued to play in his mind.

Admit it, Isandro, the kid got to you.

This perceived weakness was responsible for putting the indent between his sable brows. His father had been a sentimental man, a kind, trusting man who was moved by the suffering of others. A man who taught his son the importance of charity, and led by example.

And where had that got him?

Universally liked and admired certainly—but at the end he had been a broken and disillusioned man.

Isandro had been forced to stand by helplessly and watch while the woman his father had married and her daughter had systematically robbed the family business, stealing not just from his father but from major clients. He had no intention of emulating his parent, had no room for sentimentality in his life, expected the worst from others and was rarely disappointed.

Experience had taught him that everyone had an angle and the most innocent of faces could hide a devious heart, like his stepmother and her daughter. Forced to brake hard to avoid a cat that shot across the road out of nowhere, he shook his head, banishing the thoughts of the pair of con artists who had with clinical efficiency isolated his father, alienating him not just from trusted friends and colleagues but his family, ensuring that when Isandro had passed on the concerns expressed by senior staff it had been treated as jealous spite.

Isandro would never be the man his father had been; he'd make sure of that. The possibility that his name was synonymous with cold and heartless was to his way of thinking infinitely preferable to being considered a mug.

A faint smile flickered across his face. According to the lovely Zara he was both cold and heartless among other things. She had lost it big time and reverted to her native Russian, a language Isandro had only a smattering of, so some of the choicer insults had been lost on him, before she swept majestically out of the restaurant on her designer heels.

He exhaled, feeling a fleeting spasm of regret. The woman looked magnificent even when she was spitting fury, and the sex had been excellent.

Great sex had been about the only thing they had going for them, and it had been pretty much the perfect relationship while Zara's demands had stayed in the bedroom, but recently… He shook his head. He was not into post-mortems but if he'd lived last night again he might not have replied so honestly when Zara had pouted and asked, 'Have you listened to a word I've been saying all night?'

If he'd contented himself with an honest, no frills 'no' he might have cajoled her out of her sulks and things might not have escalated so noisily, but he hadn't. He'd irritably gone into more detail, rather unwisely revealing that he had minimal interest in shoes, the latest way to remove a skin blemish, or minor royals.

To Zara's frigid, 'I'm so sorry if I'm keeping you awake,' he had responded with an inflammatory:

'Barely.'

Zara's wrathful intake of breath had caused heads to turn and half the room had heard her hissing, 'Do you want to split up?'

The ensuing scene could have been avoided. His error of judgement had been assuming she expected to hear him say yes.

He still wasn't sure why he'd said it. It wasn't as if Zara had ever been anything but shallow, but that had never been a problem. In fact it had always suited him. It wasn't her fault that her beauty budget for a month could have paid for a disabled child's medical treatment.

Dios, but the child had really got to him, he thought, seeing not the child's face but the disapproval and contempt etched on the beautiful face of his new housekeeper.

There were no balloons along the driveway, just a peacock who sauntered across the road at a leisurely pace, forcing him to wait, then one of the team of gardeners at the wheel of a lawnmower on the now empty lawn as he drove past. Superficially at least everything was back to normal.

It wasn't until he drove into the courtyard that he realised how hard he had been searching for a legitimate cause for complaint. Frowning as much at the flash of insight as at the beat-up Transit van parked beside one of the estate Land Rovers, he opened the door and peeled out of the low-slung sports car he was driving.

He had taken a couple of steps across the cobbles when he saw a denim-clad bearded figure he assumed was the driver of the eyesore vehicle, who up to that point had been concealed from Isandro by his van.

He wasn't alone. He held in his arms a tall slender figure. Isandro stopped dead at the sight. The woman wrapped in the circle of another man's arms had her face hidden from him but the slim body was that of his housekeeper.

Anger flooded into his body, the speed and strength of the flood of emotion leaching the colour from the sculpted bones of his strong features. For the space of several heartbeats his ability to think was obliterated by pure fury as he stood with his hands clenched into fists at his sides.

As the woman emerged from the embrace, pulling away from the man's chest, he kept hold of her upper arms, saying something that made her laugh before jumping into the van and closing the door behind him with a bang.

It was the musical sound of her laughter and not the reverberating sound of the door being slammed that shook him from his fugue.

Isandro inhaled and loosened his clenched fingers. His temper had been a problem when he was a boy but he was no longer a boy—he was a man who was known for his control and objectivity.

And he had objectively wanted to drag that guy off her. It wasn't an overreaction, but a perfectly legitimate response to having his trust abused. This wasn't about a public kiss—though you had to wonder at the woman's taste. The point was this was not only his home, it was her workplace. This little scene represented a total lack of professionalism. He had given her a second chance, hoping that she would blow it, and she had not disappointed.

Feeling more comfortable having a satisfactory explanation for his moment of visceral rage, he began to walk towards her, the sound of his footsteps drowned out by the van's engine as it vanished through the arch. He knew for a fact that he did not do jealousy, especially when the woman concerned was his employee. A jealous man would not have been amused rather than angry when his lover of the moment had been caught on camera by the paparazzi being as friendly as a person could be in public without being arrested.

Waving as John's van drove away, Zoe held up her hand even after the van had vanished. Then taking a deep sustaining breath, she dropped it and turned around to face the figure she had been aware of in the periphery of her vision as John had given her a goodbye hug.

Before reaching him, her gaze swept over the low-slung powerful car parked the opposite side of the courtyard. It was a monster, low, silver and sleek. She hadn't heard it arrive but then the noise of the running engine of John's van had presumably drowned out the sound of the Spanish billionaire's arrival. It had been the prickling of the hairs on the nape of her neck that had alerted her to the presence of the tall dynamic figure as she stood there saying goodbye to John.

If she'd acknowledged him then she'd have had no choice but to introduce him to John, which was something she wanted to avoid if possible.

She had promised Chloe she'd ask him about tonight and she would. This way she could sugar-coat his response—that it would be no was a given, that he wouldn't go out of his way to frame his refusal nicely was an equally safe bet.

'Good evening. I hope you had a good journey—'

He cut across her, launching without preamble into blighting speech. 'I do not find the sight of my housekeeper with her tongue down the throat of a tradesman a particularly edifying sight. In the future I would be grateful if you kept your love life or what passes for it behind closed doors and on your own time the next time you fancy a bit of rough.'

For a second she was too startled, as much by the icy delivery as his interpretation of a simple goodbye hug, to respond to this ludicrous accusation. But when she did her voice shook with the effort to control her response. She took a deep breath and closed off her furious train of thought, tipping her head in an attitude she hoped suggested humility while she badly wanted to slap the look of smug contempt off his face.

'I'll keep that in mind when I feel the urge to force myself on some passing tradesman.' Focusing her thoughts on the price of school sports kits helped her stay calm as she levelled a clear blue gaze at his dark lean face and finished her thought. 'Though actually, for the record, on this occasion I was simply hugging a friend goodbye.' Like it's any of your business, you sanctimonious creep. 'You're right, he is a tradesman, but not rough at all,' she added, unable to keep the note of shaky indignation out of her voice. 'John is sweet.' She lifted her chin. 'And not the sort of man who judges people by appearances or what they do for a living.'

Politely framed or not, it was impossible to miss the fact he was being called a snob. For a moment Isandro was too astonished to be angry. For a long time in his life now there had been no one who would presume to tell him if he was out of line.

The moment passed and astonishment gave

way to anger that caused the muscles along his angular jaw to tighten and quiver. 'I do not care what the man does for a living!'

She arched a feathery brow and said politely, 'Of course not.'

Isandro clenched his teeth, seriously tempted to give her her marching orders and to hell with the consequences, then he recalled the delicacy of the deal on the negotiating table and the outcome was by no means a given. Any hint of scandal now would make the old family firm walk away from the table.

'What I care about is the man conducting his sex life on my doorstep!'

She stared, her blue eyes widening to their widest before narrowing into angry sparkling slits. He made it sound as if he'd discovered her having an orgy! What she couldn't understand was how could anyone have seen anything sordid in a perfectly innocent hug?

He was madder than he had been when she had given him cause. His reaction to her using his house to raise funds without his permission had been clinical, but there was nothing at all clinical about his reaction to her imagined sin now.

'The next time get a room.' The snarled suggestion triggered a free-fall avalanche of images that made him lose his thread.

'Get a room? John is married!'

His nostrils flared. 'All the more reason, I would have thought, to show a little more circumspection,' he declared austerely.

'I would not have an affair with a married man!' She took a deep breath. It really hurt to have to explain herself to this man but what choice did she have? 'What you witnessed, Mr Montero, was simply a goodbye hug between friends,' she told him stiffly. 'That was John, Chloe's husband. You remember Chloe?'

Taking his silence to be a yes, she explained further. 'He was picking up the twins. They're staying with his mother tonight. She's babysitting, because John and Chloe are having a party… you remember?'

He remembered.

'I saw—'

'You saw nothing, because there was nothing to see.'

His mind replayed the image that had caused him to jump to conclusions and he realised he had not seen anything beyond two people close. His expression froze, his discomfiture revealing itself in the faintest deepening of colour along the slashing angles of his sybaritic cheekbones. Isandro cleared his throat. Embarrassment was a foreign sensation and one he did not enjoy.

He stopped his jaw tightening. 'I apologise. I made a mistake.'

Zoe fought a smile. Clearly every syllable of his apology had hurt. 'Apology accepted. I left your mail on your desk. I wasn't sure if you wanted it forwarded. If you let me know what time is convenient I'll let the maid know when she can clean your study. Oh, and shall I let your chef know what time you'll want dinner, sir?' She took a breath and thought, Wow, I'm good.

His brows lifted. 'I assumed that we would be dining out.'

Zoe shook her head, losing control of her 'perfect housekeeper' smile. 'Dining?'

'What time did your friend say—seven?'

She gave a little laugh, her face clearing. 'The party! Oh, goodness, you don't have to come.'

'Then the invitation is not genuine?'

'Yes, it's genuine—Chloe and John are very genuine people. I just thought that under the circumstances...'

He arched a questioning brow. 'Circumstances?'

This deliberate display of obtuseness brought her full lips together in a pursing line of annoyance. 'They are going to want to thank you, and I'd assumed that you'd find that embarrassing.'

Of course her analysis was dead on, but it turned out his reluctance to attend this party was not as strong as his enthusiasm to not follow the script she clearly wanted him to.

Where women were concerned Isandro did not consider himself complacent, but neither did he anticipate rejection. It was his male pride responding, rather than common sense, as he bared his white teeth in a smile that did not reach his dark eyes and framed his silky response.

'It is always pleasant when people are grateful.' Some women would be grateful to be offered the chance of sharing an evening with him. 'You will find I'm not easily embarrassed.'

Zoe struggled to hide her dismay. 'Does that mean you want to come?'

While he knew it was illogical to put himself through what would be an uncomfortable and almost certainly boring evening, the dismay in her voice that she didn't have either the skill or the good manners to disguise hardened his stubborn resolve to attend the damned party with her at his side—and she'd damned well enjoy it! he thought.

'It's not a matter of want. I gave my word.'

She struggled to read the expression on his lean sardonic face and faltered. 'They'd understand if you...'

'What time will you pick me up?'

Zoe's heart sank to her boots and she shook her head, feigning incomprehension.

Isandro smiled. She was a very bad actress—an actress with the most incredible mouth he had ever seen.

'Was that not the arrangement—you take me…?' he asked, utilising his much more polished acting skills. 'Of course, I can arrange a driver if you have other plans.'

Her only plan at that moment was to retreat to her little flat and bang her head on a brick wall! Inevitably he would be a back-seat driver. The sinking sensation in the pit of her stomach as she thought of being forced to share such a small space with him raised goosebumps over her body, but she cheered herself with the mental image of his elegant length folded into the not at all elegant confines of her Beetle that had seen better days. She squared her slender shoulders and ran her tongue across the surface of her dry lips.

Time to accept the inevitable and make the best of the situation. She was still mystified why he would want to come. Perhaps he just enjoyed having people tell him what a great guy he was, she thought scornfully, but the reality was it was going to happen so she'd better stop fighting it and make the best of the situation. It was one evening of her life, and she was probably worrying unnecessarily—his social skills were probably not nearly as bad as she feared.

'No, that's fine. I thought I'd leave around seven, if that suits you?'

He lifted his shoulders in a fluid shrug. 'I will be waiting.'

Her brave smile tipped his emotions over into amusement tinged with determination. He had always found it hard to resist a challenge. By the time this evening was over he would have Miss Zoe Grace eating out of his hand.

CHAPTER FIVE

GIVEN THE LIMITED storage space in the flat it was lucky Zoe didn't have a lot of clothes. Those that didn't fit into the cupboard in the hallway she kept in a case under the twins' bed.

On her knees she dragged it into the middle of the room, then sat back on her heels and went through the contents. The choice did not take long as she only possessed two half-decent summer dresses. After a few moments of narrow-eyed contemplation, she chose the maxi, mainly because it had fewer creases. Putting it on a hanger she hung it over the bathroom door and turned on the shower, hoping the steam from it would smooth out the few there were in the light chiffon fabric that she was a bit nervous about pressing because she still hadn't got around to replacing her iron with its dodgy thermostat.

Fifteen minutes later, some light make-up

applied, her hair loosened from the plait and brushed into silky submission in waves that almost reached her waist, she switched off the water in the bathroom and was pleased to see that it had worked—the creases had virtually all fallen out of the misty blue fabric.

Slipping it over her head, she adjusted the shoe spaghetti straps and stooped down to get a glimpse of herself in the mirror. She hardly recognised the grave young woman who looked back at her, and allowed herself a complacent smile. When was the last time she'd dressed up? So long ago she couldn't remember. It was a shame that on this occasion she had that terrible man along for the ride.

With any luck he would get bored and leave early.

Hugging this comforting thought to herself, she walked across the courtyard back to the big house and found him waiting outside the porticoed entrance.

The sound of the fountain drowned out the noise her heels made on the cobbles, so she was able to study him unobserved for a few moments. He was wearing an open-necked shirt and dark tailored trousers. She was admiring the way he looked, hard not to, and reflecting that it was a shame that someone who had everything physically should be so lacking in the personality department when he turned suddenly, startling her enough to make her fall off the strappy wedge she was wearing.

He was at her side supplying a steadying hand to her elbow with startling speed. Flustered, she lifted her face to his, the pupils of her dramatic cornflower-blue eyes dilating as they connected with his dark ebony burnished stare.

She caught her breath sharply as a shimmy of sensation that slid down her spine made her shiver. The man had a sexual charisma that really was off the scale!

'I'm not used to the heels.' She pulled and his hand fell away from her elbow. 'I'm afraid my car's not very…' Her voice faded as she picked her way with more care now across the cobbles.

Isandro had been pierced by an arrow of sheer

lust the moment he had seen her walking towards him. Walking behind her gave him the opportunity to admire her delicious bottom and the long elegant line of her seemingly endless legs, revealed rather than hidden by the long skirt that clung and flowed as she walked.

'The seat belt's a bit...' She took the football he held and with a grimace slung it into the back seat on top of the motley collection of toys and turned the ignition. 'It takes a few times before it... Sometimes...'

'Will you stop apologising?' He nodded towards the back seat. 'Your nephew plays football?' He spoke not out of any genuine interest but a desire to stop himself asking her if she had a boyfriend. It wouldn't make a difference—she worked for him and some rules he did not break. Still, there was no rule against looking.

'Harry?' Zoe laughed and shook her head. 'No, Harry hates sport. The ball is Georgie's. Harry is...quieter.' A man like Isandro Montero would never understand a sensitive boy like Harry. Her brow furrowed. Harry was a worry; he was such an easy child that he tended to be overlooked.

She glanced towards her passenger, and her lips twitched at the thought of anyone overlooking the scorchingly handsome Spaniard. It should have been laughable to see him squashed into her Beetle, but Zoe was unable to raise even a smile. The fact they were virtually rubbing shoulders made her feel a lot less comfortable than he appeared to be.

Being in this sort of enclosed space with him made Zoe want to crawl out of her own skin.

'It's not far.' Thank God for small mercies.

'I will sit back and admire the scenery,' he said, studying her profile. He had thought she would scrub up well and he had been proved right—she was stunning.

A few minutes later she crunched the gears and winced as she drew up outside the local convenience store.

'Your friends live here?'

'No, they live the other side of the village. I need to stop to get a bottle of wine.'

'I thought you didn't drink.'

'I don't, but other people do,' she said shortly without looking at him.

'You should have said. There's plenty of wine in the cellar.' Good wine was always a sound inflation-proof investment.

A small choking sound left her lips as she thought of the vintage stuff stacked in the hall's cellar being served from borrowed glasses and drunk by people who in her hostess's case preferred her wine mixed with lemonade.

'Don't worry about it. I'll get this.'

Inside the store she snatched two of the second-cheapest bottles off the shelves and took them to the checkout.

'Nice stuff this, so they say,' the man at the till approved, putting the bottles into a bag for her while she dug into her purse. It became embarrassingly clear pretty quickly that she was short of cash to pay and her plastic was at home in the drawer, which had seemed the safest way to avoid temptation while she adjusted to her new straitened circumstances.

'Sorry, it'll have to be the Spanish one—do you mind if I change them? Fifty pence short, I'm afraid.' She nodded towards the stacked coins.

'No problem, it's very nice too, love.'

Her hand had closed around the bottles on the counter when a big hand covered it. 'Let me get those.'

Looking from the warm hand covering her own to the face of the tall, sleek, exclusive-looking man who had moved to stand beside her, Zoe shook her head, struggling to recover her composure and painfully aware of the tingling pain in her peaked and aching nipples. She was shamed and embarrassed by her weakness.

'No, really, I'm fine. I'm going to have the Spanish one…wine, that is…' she corrected and promptly felt like a total idiot.

'I hate to be disloyal, but take it from a Spaniard—that is not wine,' he told her with a shudder.

'It's not a wine snob sort of party.'

He was prepared to swallow the insult, but not the wine on the shelf. 'No, I insist, the least I can do since you are being my taxi,' he said, taking his wallet from his pocket and handing over the money.

Short of having a fight right there in the shop, Zoe had no choice but to accept the offer with as much grace as possible.

With his hand on the small of her back he guided her out of the shop and back towards the car. She didn't enjoy the light physical contact—actually any contact at all with this man made her feel uncomfortable—but she could tell that the natural courtesy came as second nature to him.

He held the door open for her, then went around to the other side of the car. The entire vehicle shook as she slammed the door closed. 'Do you not drink out of choice or because you have a drink problem?'

Her lips tightened. Was the man worried that his new housekeeper was an alcoholic? 'Neither, sir.' She emphasised the title before adding factually, 'I simply can't metabolise alcohol. I get drunk on the smell.'

'I rather think it might be more appropriate if you do not call me sir tonight.'

She shrugged and steered her car past the others parked along one side of the narrow lane. 'Is that an order, Mr Montero?'

'If you like, and try Isandro. It is my name. Relax,' he recommended. 'This is a party. I will not cramp your style...'

'It's not that sort of party and be careful there's a...' She stopped and hid a smile, adding as he surveyed his muddy shoe, 'A bit of a ditch that side.'

Zoe had been concerned for her friends' feelings, but slowly let down her guard as she realised that, far from looking down his nose at her friends, he was charming them. She could relax and enjoy herself; why not? Against all her expectations he was not being aloof or even icily polite. From the moment they had arrived and he had been swept away by Chloe, who had wanted to show him off, he had given the appearance of enjoying himself.

Watching Isandro talk easily with John and the

local vet—who, according to Chloe, had not worn low-cut blouses before her divorce—it was Zoe who found herself feeling like an outsider. She felt her resentment rise as the red-headed divorcee threw back her head and laughed throatily at something Isandro had said, giving him an excellent view of her cleavage. Zoe's teeth clenched—and he looked, of course; he was a man!

How predictable. Shaking her head in a combination of contempt and cynical amusement, she felt embarrassed for the woman who was being so obvious. And he wasn't doing anything to discourage her, she thought. Her eyes narrowed as the woman's hand came to rest on his arm and stayed there, her long nails showing as flashes of scarlet as they curved over his biceps.

Zoe couldn't decide if the woman was pathetic or predatory…and whether she herself was embarrassed or envious.

Ignoring the laughable possibility that she wanted to touch Isandro, she directed her stubbornly critical glance over his strong, arrogant profile, pushing away the image of moving her hands over the hard muscular contours of his body, waiting for the hot hormone rush that tinged her cheek with pink to recede.

This was insane, she told herself. How could the man be all the way over the other side of the room and still manage to jangle every nerve ending in her body? His masculinity really was totally overwhelming. She sipped her drink, wishing that there were something stronger than fruit juice in it—though maybe not; the last thing she needed was her social restraints vanishing. Zoe had not exaggerated when she explained her reaction to alcohol; she had learnt after a couple of deeply embarrassing experiences that she and booze were not a good combination.

Common sense told her this was about hormones. She'd just have to accept it as an uncomfortable fact, like a pollen allergy, and deal with it. No point whatsoever in overanalysing the primitive physical response he had awoken in her, and it didn't really matter if this was all about timing or that he had been the catalyst for kicking her dormant hormones into life. She would treat it as an inconvenience rather than a disaster. There were always coping mechanisms and for the rare occasions there weren't, you avoided the problem. Like her body's inability to cope with alcohol—she didn't touch it; she wasn't going to touch Isandro. Simple.

What would be a disaster or at least an un-wanted distraction would be to think too much about the primitive hunger she sensed was some-where inside her. She should acknowledge it and forget about it. She was human; she had rotten taste in men. But she must not go there.

The vet, on the other hand, had clearly no such qualms about going where God knew how many women had been before, Zoe thought, her lips moving in a grimace of distaste as the older woman and her curves moved in closer. She had all but trapped him in the corner now…not that he showed any inclination to escape.

Her lips were still tightened in a cynical sneer of superiority when, without warning, Isandro turned his head slowly as though sensing her scrutiny. His dark eyes sought and connected with hers across the room. It was as if he possessed some radar that told him exactly where she was standing...where she was staring.

Their eyes locked, and for a long, heart-thudding moment Zoe could feel her own pulse over every inch of her skin, the vibrations reaching her tingling fingertips. She stopped breathing. Her stomach muscles quivered; her legs felt weak and oddly heavy; her knees literally shook.

The contact might have lasted moments or an hour, she didn't have a clue, but by the time she managed to bring her lashes down in a protective fan her insides had dissolved. Her throat was dry as she raised her empty glass to her lips and struggled to regain some semblance of self-control.

She closed her eyes, her lashes brushing her cheeks. As she willed her body to relax they shot open at the sound of her name.

'Sorry, I was miles away. How are you?' she asked Chloe's elderly aunt who was lowering her bulk into a chair.

'I can't complain, but of course I do. Thank

you, dear,' she added as Zoe retrieved her stick that had fallen to the floor. 'Unless you want your man going home with someone else I'd get over there, Zoe.'

Blushing, Zoe followed the direction of the old lady's sharp-eyed stare to where Isandro stood, looking like the personification of a predatory male. And the hunter was still being hunted, she saw, her mouth twisting as she watched the red-head lean into him and stroke his sleeve. 'I'm his taxi, not his date. He's my boss.'

'In my day it was most girls' dream to marry their boss. I did—not, of course, that George ever looked like that.' She saw Zoe's expression and gave a chuckle, adding, 'I'm old, child, not blind.'

'And I'm not thinking of getting married.'

If she ever did it would not be to a man like Isandro Montero, she thought, summoning a mental picture of a man who would treat her as an equal, a man who would love the twins as much as she did. Her brow furrowed as her employer's face superimposed itself over her mental image, causing her eyes to drift across the room to where…he was no longer standing, and neither was the voluptuous vet.

Maybe she wouldn't have to put up with his aggravating company on the return journey…?

'Very wise. Of course, in my day it was different. You couldn't have sex outside marriage…if you were a nice girl, that is. We didn't have your freedom.'

'Actually, I don't believe in casual sex. Not for me anyway.'

Zoe was wondering why she felt the totally uncharacteristic need to discuss her feelings on the subject, when she realised that the old lady was not looking at her, but past her.

Her stomach quivered; she knew without turning who was standing there. Had he heard what she'd said?

His expression told her nothing.

'I was wondering if you are ready to go home?'

'I thought you'd already left.'

'What gave you that idea?'

'You make friends very easily.' The moment the remark left her lips she regretted it. She glanced guiltily over her shoulder to where a distinctive throaty laugh placed the vet. The woman had by all accounts been dumped by her husband of fifteen years for a younger model. Who only knew what insecurities her flirtatious behaviour masked?

Zoe felt a stab of shame. The woman was vulnerable and needed sympathy, not catty remarks behind her back. She actually deserved admiration—she had come out fighting after being kicked in the teeth.

'Actually, I don't.'

The comment brought her attention back to the tall Spaniard. It was clear he had not been canvassing the sympathy vote, simply stating a fact.

'I think you've made a few today.' Not a single person she had spoken to had had a bad word to say about him, and several had told her how lucky she was to be working for him.

Frankly, all the rave reviews were beginning to grate. People were so superficial they didn't look past the handsome face, perfect body and incredible smile. How many people but her had noticed him empty his glass of wine into the pot plant? Possibly the ones who hadn't taken their eyes off him all night? No, they acted as if he'd done them a favour by deigning to show up.

Zoe had been forced to bite her tongue on several occasions. She'd hoped he'd behave well and not upset anyone but she hadn't bargained on him turning the entire community into his devoted fans, who wouldn't believe that the man had sacked her within two minutes of setting eyes on her, that he was still looking for an excuse. Oh, yeah, he really was a great guy!

Friendship required trust. Isandro did not consider his inability to trust easily a character flaw; rather he valued his true friends all the more because he knew how rare they were.

His eyes brushed her face and he was struck again by the directness of her blue stare. 'I have many acquaintances, but few friends.'

And you're not even an acquaintance, Zoe. You're an employee. The taxi driver, not the date. 'I suppose it's difficult to tell if someone loves you or your bank balance.'

'I do not require love.' His brows lifted. 'Or are you talking about sex?'

'Sex?'

By some horrid twist of fate her yelped echo coincided with a lull in the conversation.

Oh, let me die now, Zoe thought as everyone turned to look at her.

'Strange how that always happens.'

'Not to me, it doesn't.' She struggled to see him as gaffe prone. 'If you'll excuse me, I see...' She made a vague gesture and headed across the room, accepting a few good-natured teasing comments as she went.

'What I need,' she muttered, 'is to cool down.'

'God, yes, it's warm in here, isn't it? Try one of these.' Once again her comment had reached more than its target audience—herself.

She looked at the tall glass that clinked with ice in her hand, and opened her mouth to ask the person with the tray what it was, but he was gone.

Walking out through the open French windows, she sniffed it warily before picking out a floating strawberry to taste. The overwhelming flavour over and above the fruit was pineapple. It seemed innocuous enough, and a tentative sip reinforced this analysis. Satisfied it was one of the delicious mocktails that Chloe had made, she took a swallow.

She passed a group of men chatting, then wandered out onto the steep sloped lawn shaded by a row of tall oak trees in the field beyond. She sat down on the stump of a recently felled tree and swallowed some more of the fruit concoction. It was actually so delicious it made you wonder why people bothered with alcohol.

Tipping her head back to look at the starry sky, she thought that a person really should stop occasionally and just enjoy being alive. Lie on the grass and feel the earth…and why not?

Lying flat on her back, staring up at the stars, she began to hum a little tune softly to herself before she closed her eyes. Did she drift off?

'I can't, I really can't take this…' She half lifted her head at the sound of John's voice. Why was he ignoring her? She let out a small giggle and thought, Because he can't see me! I'm lying down.

'Yes, you can. Just think how much better it will be for Chloe and Hannah if they have you there to support them.'

This deeper voice with the sexy accent—she recognised that, too!

John and Isandro.

'I don't know what to say.' There was the sound of crinkling paper and a gasp. 'Hell, that's too much…no…I couldn't.'

'All tax-deductible. The only thing is that I'd prefer this was private between you and Chloe and me. I'm not comfortable with…'

'Understood. We won't forget this.'

Zoe lay there turning the conversation over in her head. It took her foggy brain a little while to process what she had overheard, but when she did tears of emotion sprang to her eyes. Isandro had just given John the money he needed to join his family in Boston—and more than enough, by the sound of it.

'That is so, so incredibly lovely!'

Isandro turned in time to see a figure rise from

the mist, hovering over the grass at ground level like some sort of spectral vision.

'Zoe, what were you—?' The glorious goddess-like figure flew towards him like a heat-seeking missile. *Madre di Dios*, she was plastered!

'I heard everything, and I think you're w… won…marvellous,' she declared earnestly.

'I think you should sit down.'

'I will, but first…' Standing on her tiptoes, she reached up and took his face between her hands. 'You're a very beautiful man and I've been mean to you, very very very mean. I'm so ashamed! But that's all over. You're a hero.' She leaned in closer, her soft breasts crushing against the barrier of his chest as she fitted her mouth to his.

The warm, soft mouth that pressed against his tasted of booze. Standing rigid, his hands wide, he knew if he touched that body, drunk or not, he would not be able to stop himself having her right there on the grass. He somehow managed to resist the blandishments of those luscious lips.

The effort brought a sheen of sweat to his skin and a great deal of pain to his groin, but he held out. Though the throaty little mewling sound of complaint she made in her throat when he didn't respond almost broke him.

'I think…I think I might sit down.' Clutching her head, and without warning, she sank gracefully to the grass and sat there cross-legged.

Isandro sighed and picked up the almost empty glass he saw there. He dipped his finger in the contents and licked it. A lot of fruit juices and vodka. Not a lot, but it was there.

Behind him he heard Chloe and John approach. 'Is that Zoe?'

'Hi, guys…yes, it's Zoe,' Zoe said, waving her hand. 'Chloe, you musht give me the recipe for that mocktail.'

'Oh, God!' Chloe gasped.

'He's not a monster, Chloe, he's a hero—did you know that? A real-life hero. He doesn't like me, though…sad.'

Isandro handed John the glass. 'It's pretty innocuous.'

'It doesn't matter. It's a metabolic thing with Zoe—she couldn't have known. What are we going to do with her? We've got a full house to-night, not even a spare sofa.'

Isandro saw them both looking at him.

Isandro, who never did anything he did not want to, heard himself say, 'I'll take her home. Don't worry, I've not been drinking.'

Once they got her in the car she immediately went to sleep curled up like a kitten, her mouth slightly open.

'Will she remember when she sobers up?'

'Oh, yes,' said Chloe, a wave of sadness crossing her face. 'Or that's what Laura always said.'

Isandro nodded. He was pleased with the reply. It only seemed fair that she would remember, because he surely would. It was hard to forget the extremely painful cost of being a hero; he was pretty sure that the resulting frustration would cost him a night's sleep.

Zoe continued to sleep like a baby all the way back to the hall, which was good because he wasn't sure his response would be quite so noble if she made another attempt to jump him.

When he opened the passenger door the cool

night air woke her. He was amazed and relieved that she had recovered enough to make it up the stone steps to the flat without any assistance from him, but he followed behind just in case.

'You'll be all right?'

She looked at him blearily. 'I think there was something in my drink.'

'Vodka.'

'Oh, God! I thought it… Sorry…' She had no idea what she was apologising for, but it seemed safe to assume that there was something. 'Goodnight, Mr Montero.'

Isandro watched the door close. He was quite pleased with his demotion back to monster. Monsters were not obliged to behave with honour—they could take what they wanted.

CHAPTER SIX

ROBBED OF HIS early morning ride after discovering his horse had pulled a shoe, Isandro returned to the house, leaving the stallion in the capable hands of his groom. An hour on a cross-trainer in the gym did not really touch his frustration levels.

Heading downstairs after his shower, he reached the galleried landing when he almost fell over her.

'What the hell are you doing?' If she appeared at all this morning he had imagined she would be nursing a hangover, not on her knees singing to herself.

Seemingly oblivious to his presence, she continued to bang the hand-held vacuum into a crevice under a console table, still humming along to the music playing in her ears. Her singing voice was totally flat but her behind was not. Isandro, who had opened his mouth to deliver his demand again, closed it as she reached further forward, the action causing her delightful bottom to tighten against the pair of jeans she was wearing.

Lust hit him like a hammer blow to the chest. Beside his sensual mouth a nerve quivered, beating out an erratic tattoo as in his head he saw himself dropping down beside her, tipping her onto her back… His chest lifted as he sucked in a deep breath and swore through gritted teeth. He had never experienced this degree of blind, relentless lust before. Not even in his teens had he felt so obsessed.

He swore under his breath and bellowed, 'What the hell are you doing?'

One hand on the floor to steady herself, Zoe turned her head, a questioning furrow in her smooth brow. She saw Isandro and her half-smile faded with a speed that under other circumstances he might have found amusing.

'It is always nice when people are glad to see me,' he muttered under his breath.

'Pardon…' Zoe lowered her voice, murmuring a self-conscious, 'Sorry.' She pulled the earphones out of her ears and looked up at the figure who towered over her. 'I didn't see you there.' She stopped herself from asking whether there was anything she could do for him, afraid that he might tell her—and even more afraid that she might deliver his request.

She was probably worrying over nothing. Last night he hadn't even kissed her back.

It was the ultimate humiliation. She had offered herself up on a platter and he had said no, thank you, and she remembered every mortifying, cringeworthy detail. It had been about three a.m. when she'd sat bolt upright in bed and it had all come rushing back to her.

Unable to resist the masochistic compulsion to relive the scene over and over, by this morning she didn't see how she could face him. And now it felt just as awful as she had imagined.

Should she mention last night? Wait for him to? Or should she pretend it never happened?

'I said what the hell are you doing?'

'I'm vacuuming the carpet.' She held out the hand-held vacuum she was using to reach the crevices, flicking the switch into the on position to demonstrate as she got up from her knees.

'I can see what you're doing.' He reached over and flicked the switch off. 'What I want to know is why?'

'Susie couldn't come in this morning.'

'That does not answer my question, and who the hell is Susie?'

'Susie is one of the cleaning staff. She lives in the village.'

He folded his arms across his chest and looked unimpressed by her explanation. 'Will you stop waving that thing at me?'

Zoe lowered the vacuum, but lifted her free hand to shade her eyes from the shaft of strong morning sun that shone in from the tall floor-length window behind Isandro, framing his tall figure in a golden haze of light. As if he needed any help to look as though he'd just stepped down from Mount Olympus! It was like a massive conspiracy to turn her into some sex-starved bimbo.

'You're really not a morning person, are you?'

A gleam flashed in his dark eyes. 'I've never had any complaints.'

It took a few seconds, but when the penny dropped her face flamed. She brought down her lashes in a protective sweep to shield her eyes. Head down, she swept off the scarf she had tied over her hair. Ruffling it with her hand as it slipped down her back, she struggled to maintain a professional attitude given the reel of lurid images now playing in her head.

Isandro felt the hunger flare, his body hardening as he watched the river of glossy silk settle down her narrow back. The sexy little black outfit was gone and she was back in jeans, complete with a tear in one knee and belt loops he could have hooked his fingers into and jerked her... The effort to suppress his lustful imagination drew a short harsh rasp from his throat.

'This still doesn't tell me why I find you down on your hands and knees like some...'

Her head lifted; her blue eyes shone with anger. 'Servant?' she bit back. 'Maybe because I am.'

'You are the housekeeper.'

She shrugged, not sure why he was making such a big thing of this. It wasn't as if the workings of a vacuum cleaner were alien to her. 'Call it multitasking...'

'I call it inappropriate. What sort of first impression would it give if I had walked in with a group of important guests and the first thing they see is the housekeeper down on her knees?' He shook his head.

'You didn't walk in with...'

Isandro's expression made her wish she had held her tongue.

'It is totally inappropriate to your position here.'

'What was I meant to do? Drag poor Susie in with her abscessed tooth? Her mother says the poor girl is in agony.'

'You were meant to delegate.' It amazed him that she had not grasped this basic precept.

'I don't like telling people what to do.' Zoe found it was easier and less stressful to do things herself.

'Delegation is part of your job. Scrubbing floors is not.'

His coldness hit her like a slap in the face. 'I wasn't…' She bit her tongue and bowed her head.

The show of humility did not fool Isandro for one second. He knew full well it was an act. She was about as humble as a battle cruiser.

'Part of your job is also learning the difference between showing sympathy and being a soft touch.'

Zoe's head lifted at the suggestion. 'I'm not a soft touch!' she protested indignantly.

'People take advantage of you.' His annoyance that she was either unable or unwilling to see this was etched on his hard features.

'You didn't!' She closed her eyes and lifted a hand to her head, let her chin fall to her chest and thought, Please let me die now. 'Sorry. I didn't mean to say that. It just sort of slipped out.'

'Not because I did not want to, if that is what is bothering you. Did you get any sleep?' The violet smudges under her eyes showed up clear against her translucent skin, as did the handful of freckles across the bridge of her nose.

She nodded. 'And I woke with a bit of a head-ache.'

His mobile lips twitched. 'Called a hangover.'

Zoe shuddered as she got to her feet. 'I can't imagine why people drink.'

'Not everyone has your zero tolerance. For some people it's their drug of choice, and it's legal.'

'What's yours, or don't you need one? Sorry...I keep forgetting... Can I take your order for dinner, sir?'

'You can't go from trying to kiss my face off to calling me sir. Neither are what I expect of my housekeeper. I will settle for a happy medium.'

The mortified colour rushed to her cheeks as she pressed her teeth into her full lower lip. 'I am sorry for last night. I really am. But what you did for Chloe and John, that was...very kind.'

His features froze. 'That stays within these walls. Is that understood?'

Before she could reply to this terse warning,

the front door swung open and the twins rushed in. At least Georgie rushed. Harry walked with his nose in a book.

'No, not here. I've told you, the flat—'

'We know. You forgot to put the key under the mat.' Georgie looked at Isandro and grinned. 'We have to keep out of your way.' She wrinkled her nose. 'Don't you like kids?'

'It depends on the kid.' He strolled across to the boy, a skinny child with strawberry-blond hair. 'You're Harry.'

Harry nodded.

'Run along, children.' She pulled the key fob out of her pocket and tossed it to Georgie. 'I've left you some sandwiches for eleven. I'll be over at lunchtime.'

'What's that you're reading?' Isandro looked at the title on the spine. 'You like the stars?'

Of course he did. Skinny, undersized boys with books and no friends always did. Isandro knew because he had been one himself. In his case he had grown twelve inches at sixteen and gone from being the despised wimp to the jock that everybody wanted to know.

Harry nodded, his face suffused with pink.

'On the wall on my desk I have a photo of the Horsehead nebula. Have you seen it?'

'We're not allowed in the house. Especially your office.' So Harry was not a rule-breaker. 'I like looking at the night sky, but I want to be an astrophysicist when I grow up.'

Zoe blinked. This was news to her.

'Cool,' Isandro said.

'Run along, children.' She was both pleased and relieved when they both did as she asked— with Georgie, you never knew.

'You, too,' Isandro said when they had left. 'Ring the agency first and get a replacement for… whatever her name is.'

'Susie.'

'Then take the rest of the day off. I'm off to London.'

She assumed when he left that they would not see him for some time. She had understood that this was the norm. But over the next few weeks he kept arriving unexpectedly, sometimes spending a night, sometimes not even that long.

At first mystified by his behaviour, she realised that he was hoping to catch her out, though it did seem a lot of trouble to go to. Never knowing when he would turn up made it difficult to relax…and though trying to catch her out made sense, it didn't explain the occasion he brought Harry a book full of photos of galaxies and nebulae.

The little boy looked forward to his visits…but was he the only one? Why would anyone look forward to a visit from someone who blew hot and cold? Who was cold and remote one moment and relaxed and friendly the next?

As they approached the crossroad Alex slowed for a red light. Isandro shut down the tablet and looked through the window, dragging a hand through his dark hair. He had planned to spend the weekend in London, but at the last moment had decided to drive down to Ravenwood, reasoning he could spend the weekend reading the report without distractions. Sure, no distractions at all, mocked the voice in his head.

'Is that…?'

Pushing away the thought, Isandro followed the direction of his driver's nod. 'Yes, it is, Alex,' he confirmed.

'Are they alone?'

Isandro, who had been looking for that glossy dark head attached to a body he had spent some time thinking about, nodded. All right, not just some time—a lot of time. He was finding it pretty much impossible to think about anything but his housekeeper, who did not know the meaning of 'unobtrusive'.

'It looks like it.'

Which in itself was strange. While Zoe Grace might not be about to win any prizes for her housekeeping skills, when it came to her youthful charges she took the role extremely seriously. He could not imagine her allowing the twins to wander around town unaccompanied.

'Shall I pull over?'

Isandro nodded and unclipped his seat belt as the car drew to a halt on a double yellow. When he reached the twins they were still on the pavement. They appeared to be arguing—and more significantly there was still no sign of their aunt.

It was Harry who saw him first. Seeing the relief on his freckled face, Isandro experienced an emotional tightening in his chest.

Isandro controlled his strong inclination to hug him, aware that the boy had already measured him up as an unlikely male role model. It would be nothing short of cruel to allow the boy to become reliant and then fade out of his life.

Instead he gave the boy a manly pat on his painfully skinny shoulder. The kid could do a lot better than him for a father substitute. Did his aunt's determination to sacrifice her own needs for her charges extend to her choice of partner? Would she choose the 'good father' material over a good lover? The woman was probably determined to be a martyr. She'd probably end up alone or with some boring loser whom she deemed solid and responsible.

'We've lost Aunty Zoe. Actually, we ran away and now we're lost, too.'

For which Isandro correctly read his sister had run and he had followed. There was no doubting who the dominant and reckless twin in this equation was.

'We're not lost,' his sister interrupted. 'And if you hadn't made me come back...'

'It was stealing!'

'It was not stealing. We were bringing it back, and that's borrowing, isn't it?' she appealed to Isandro for support.

'Borrowing without permission is stealing. And running away from your aunt is... Have you any idea how worried she will be?' An image of a terrified Zoe flashed into his head and he hardened his heart against their stricken expressions. 'She will be frantic!'

The twins exchanged worried glances.

'We didn't think,' Georgie admitted.

Isandro steeled himself against the quiver in her voice and struggled to maintain his stern expression as he ushered them towards the car. The sniff was too much for the ruthless captain of industry to withstand.

'Don't worry,' he soothed. 'I'll ring your aunt and let her know—'

'You can't,' they said in unison.

He shook his head. 'Why can't I?'

'Her phone wasn't charged. It died on her when Aunt Chloe was talking.'

He exhaled. If he had been in Zoe's position—which was unlikely, because not only would he not have let his phone battery run down, he certainly wouldn't have taken on responsibility for this pair of demons—he would now be retracing his footsteps.

The demons regarded him with the expressions that said they had total faith that he would come up with a solution.

'Right, then, where were you when you ran away, and where were you before that?'

The terrible clawing panic in her stomach when she had turned to tell the twins to get a wriggle or the car would be clamped would stay with Zoe for ever. When she found them she would never let them out of her sight again…always supposing she didn't throttle them.

She jogged along the pavements, retracing her footsteps, stopping occasionally to ask people if they had seen two children, oblivious to the stares that followed her progress. She kept telling herself over and over like a mantra, *Tomorrow this will just be a memory. I'll laugh about it with Chloe.*

Tomorrow seemed a hell of a long way away, though, and Chloe was still in Boston!

By the time Zoe had worked her way to the boat-hire booth her heart was thudding so hard she felt as if it would crack her ribs. She was only kept going by the strong conviction that had gradually taken hold that the twins were out there on the river.

It was so obvious. Why hadn't she smelt a rat when the wilful youngster who would never take no for an answer had not argued or even tried to cajole when she'd refused to take them out in a kayak. Now of course it made sense. Georgie hadn't suddenly become malleable, she'd simply cut out the arguing, and she'd dragged Harry with her.

The ticket booth was closed, but before a frantic Zoe could think of what to do next a boy came around the corner carrying a padlock and a large bunch of keys. He removed the earphones from his ears when he saw her.

'Sorry, we're closed.'

'I'm looking for my niece and nephew,' she said before he could put the earphones back in. 'They're seven years old. I think they might have gone out in one of your kayaks.' The effort to stay calm and not sound like an unbalanced lunatic made her voice shake, but she was pretty proud of her effort.

'Sorry, we're closed.'

She watched, her pent-up fear tipping over into rage, as he began to insert the earphones.

Her eyes narrowed, she stepped forward and snatched them out, drawing a yelp from the boy. 'My niece and nephew—they wanted to go out in a kayak. Have you seen them?' she yelled, fighting the impulse to shake the information from the stupid boy who was backing away from her.

'I don't know what your problem is, miss, but the public are not allowed here. There's a sign. It's health and safety.' He pointed to a no-entry sign on the wall of the booth.

Give me strength! 'I've been trying to tell you what the problem is. I'm looking for two children, a boy and girl. So high…' She held her palm at the appropriate height. 'They wanted to go out…' She closed her eyes, seeing Georgie's expression when she had refused their request. God, but she really should have seen this coming. 'I think they might be out there.' She swallowed as her eyes moved to the horizon where the grey water of the river met the darker grey sky. 'In one of your canoes.'

'No children allowed in the kayaks without a responsible adult. Besides, we're closing early— there's a storm coming.' His phone rang and he wandered away with it pressed to his ear.

When Zoe took the situation into her own hands the youth was close enough for her to hear him say, 'No way…outside the pub at five.' But not close enough, thanks to a tree, for him to see her wade into the shallow water and push out a stray canoe that had not yet been dragged onto the artificial beach.

She'd been kayaking before, she reminded herself as she managed on the third try to clamber into the swaying boat. Of course on that occasion Laura had been paddling, and she'd been only five years old, but this was a detail. How hard could it be?

Five minutes later Zoe had gone several hundred yards. But she had no idea whether she was heading in the right direction. She didn't have the faintest idea where they were! She was acting on intuition, but wasn't that another name for blind panic?

She squared her shoulders and dipped her oar into the water. She had to stay positive.

The obvious sensible thing to do would have been to go to the police…so why was she just realising that now when she was literally up the creek? Then the rain started.

The downpour was of biblical flood proportions. Within two minutes she was drenched. Her hair plastered against her skull; the water streamed down her face, making it hard to see. More worrying than her wet clothes was the water sloshing around in the bottom of the canoe.

Trying to see past the rain that was now being driven horizontally by a gale-force wind into her face, she recalled the weather man's prediction of light showers and laughed.

The hysterical sound was whipped away by the wind, which was again blowing her in the wrong direction. Head bent, she paddled hard but, despite the fact her arms felt as though they were falling off, she made no headway. She put oar down for a moment to ease the burning pain in the muscles of her upper arms and shoulders, flexing her stiff fingers as she balanced it across the canoe.

She saw it happening as if in slow motion. She lunged forward, one arm outstretched and the other holding onto the edge of the wildly rocking kayak. Just as her fingers touched the oar a current carried it away out of reach. Her centre of gravity lost, Zoe struggled to pull back, but just when it seemed inevitable she would be pitched into the grey swirling water she managed to recover, collapsing back with a sob of laughing relief into the canoe.

It hardly seemed possible that a couple of weeks ago she had decided that this stretch of the river, with its series of shallow waterfalls and half-submerged stone slabs where people sunbathed and children paddled in shallow pools, made for a really lovely afternoon stroll. Pretty, but not dramatic.

Today it did not lack drama. The river was wild white water, full of dark swirls and hidden obstacles. The boulders she strove to avoid were only just visible above the foaming white water. Zoe paddled with her hands but soon recognised it was hopeless. The kayak would never survive.

Feeling surprisingly calm in the face of impending disaster, Zoe was in the middle of telling herself she was overreacting when the kayak hit a submerged rock. The jarring motion as it

glanced off sent the flimsy craft rocking sideways. Thrown off balance, Zoe lurched sideways,
throwing her body weight sharply to one side to
right the canoe. For a moment it seemed to work,
but it was hit by an extra-strong squall of wind
and simply carried on going.

This time there was no reprieve and the immersion in the shockingly cold grey water took
her breath. For a moment she panicked, flailing
around blindly as she tried to free herself from
the upturned canoe, hampered by clothes that
dragged her downwards. When she did she surfaced almost immediately, choking as she gasped
for air. Behind her the canoe was making its way
upside down through the churning white water,
before it vanished over the top of a weir.

That could have been me.

But it won't be. The twins would be all alone,
they need me. Focusing on that one thought and
not the cold seeping into her bones, she struck
out strongly, aiming for the opposite bank, where
she would be likely to see someone who could
raise the emergency services. Zoe was a strong

swimmer with no fear of the water, but even so the going was tough and her progress, hampered by her clothes, was torturously slow.

As she swam she was distantly aware of a sound above the echoing roar of the water and her own heartbeat but she didn't allow it to distract her. She couldn't stop. She had to keep going. Every second she wasted the twins could be… No, she wouldn't think like that. She needed to focus.

'Focus, Zoe,' she said to herself—but the water filled her open mouth and, choking, her head went under.

As she was lifted unceremoniously out of the water she continued to kick feebly, right up to the moment she was hauled over and left utterly disorientated in an inelegant heap in the bottom of what seemed to be a small motorboat.

She grunted as the boat swerved, sharply throwing her against a wooden seat. The locker underneath was open and a child's inflatable vest spilled out. Oh, God, the children were out there somewhere!

She began to cry great silent, gulping sobs that racked her entire body.

Once the boat was away from the immediate danger of hitting the rocks and in the relative safety of open water, Isandro cut back on the throttle and turned his attention to the sodden bundle of misery sitting in the bottom of the boat.

He experienced a gripping sensation in his chest almost as strong as the one he had felt when he had seen her head vanish under the grey water—though without the soul-destroying terror.

'What the hell did you think you were doing?' he blasted.

She recognised the voice but was convinced she was dreaming. Except in her dreams he hadn't sounded angry... Zoe dragged her hair back from her face. My God, it was him!

It was Isandro! Looking furious, very wet and not dressed for sailing!

'Isandro...how...?' She stopped. It didn't matter how he came to be here. 'No,' she croaked, grabbing at his leg and tugging. 'I've got to go back.'

'You want me to throw you back in the water?

Do not tempt me,' he growled, seeing her vanish beneath the grey water again and feeling the visceral kick of fear in his gut again. He never wanted to relive the moment when he saw her go under.

'No, Isandro, you don't understand! I think the twins…'

Some of the anger died from his face as he placed his hands on her shoulders and dragged her up onto the wooden bench seat beside him. Shaking so hard that her teeth chattered, she transferred her desperate grip to his jacket. Frantic to communicate the urgency of the situation, she grabbed his lapels and pulled.

'The twins—'

'No, Zoe—'

'Listen, will you?'

He caught hold of her hands. 'The twins are with Alex, who is not, I admit, the most likely child-minder. In fact it is highly likely that he is even now teaching them to play poker. But they are safe.'

Zoe blinked as she shook her head, trying to

clear the fog in her brain. Why couldn't she think straight?

'The twins are all right?' Without waiting for a reply, she pushed her head into his chest and began to cry in earnest.

His arms went out wide as he looked down at the head of tangled hair. His anger had vanished and he refused to recognise the feelings that had rushed in to fill the vacuum as tenderness. Her cries tore at him; finally the mewling sounds as she burrowed in deeper snapped his resistance and his arms closed around her. He lifted her body into the warmth of his.

'*Madre di Dios*, you're an imbecile, a raving... You make me want, you make me feel—' He stopped and thought, you make me feel...too much. Digging his fingers into her wet hair, he stroked her scalp and let her cry herself out.

He had stopped resisting the sexual desire he felt for her. Physical desire was normal, not complicated. It was something that he understood and accepted, not a weakness. It did not require that he surrender any control; it was not about trusting. He wanted her on his terms—he would have her on his terms. He would not fall into the trap of allowing emotions to cloud his judgement.

He was not his father.

Finally peeling herself away, Zoe straightened up, blinking like someone waking up.

'I'm...' She gulped and shook her head again as he removed his jacket and draped it around her shoulders.

'It's wet but better than nothing.'

The lining was still warm. 'Sorry,' she said, not meeting his eyes. She was too embarrassed by her total meltdown. Why did she always make a total fool of herself around him?

He kept one hand on her shoulder, the other on the tiller, guiding the boat towards the mooring.

'Sorry...I...I thought...' Her lips quivered as she struggled for composure. 'I thought they'd gone on the river...' She gave a frown, trying to remember the sequence of events as much for her own benefit as for his. 'We'd been to the craft fair in the park. When we started back it was late and I thought they were with me. I was running—

they were going to clamp the car...' Wrong tense, she realised, they probably already had clamped the car. But having faced what she had thought was a real disaster, car clamping faded into insignificance.

She pushed the wet strands of hair from her eyes and pressed the heels of both hands to her temples before slowly turning her head to stare at him.

'What the hell made you go out on the water? Are you suicidal?'

'The twins—'

'And what would have happened to the twins if you had drowned?' Her horrified little gasp felt like a knife sliding between his ribs, but Isandro didn't allow his expression to soften as Zoe went several shades whiter. The only colour in her face was her dramatic sapphire eyes and the blue discoloration around her lips.

'I was not going to drown,' she protested through chattering teeth.

Faced with this refusal to acknowledge, let alone show any remorse for, the total bloody selfishness of her reckless actions, Isandro was tempted to throw her back in the water.

'My mistake,' he gritted through clenched teeth. 'I can see now that you had the situation totally under control.'

Unable to tear her eyes off the nerve that was throbbing in his lean cheek, she shook her head. 'No, really, I'm a strong swimmer...obviously I'm grateful but...'

'But really you didn't need my help at all.' He gave a shrug and, cutting the engine, steered the gliding boat expertly between the moored vessels.

Before Zoe could respond he leapt out of the boat, landing lithely on the wooden pier where he proceeded to tie off the boat.

'I really am grateful, Isandro. It was really lucky you had a boat.'

'I don't have a boat.' A faint smile flickered across his face. 'Not here anyway.'

'But this?' The boat wobbled as she got to her feet. With a grimace Zoe sat down again abruptly.

Her knees were still shaking and she had no desire to repeat her earlier immersion.

Considering the question, Isandro thought of Georgie's defence and smiled to himself. 'I borrowed it.'

'You stole it!' she cried, but then, not wanting to come across as ungrateful again, she added, 'But I suppose it was an emergency.'

'What made you think they were heading for the river?'

'Georgie wanted to go out in a canoe and I said no. We really didn't have time...'

'You do not have to justify your decisions to me, Zoe.'

'Georgie is...'

'Determined?'

Zoe acknowledged the dry suggestion with a shrug. 'She didn't fight it, which isn't like her. Saying no is like a red rag to her. I should have known.' After a fractional pause that was not lost on Isandro, she accepted the hand he held out to her and rose unsteadily to her feet. The boat swayed again and she lurched, making an awkward leap as he tugged.

As she landed clumsily on the boarded walkway Zoe heard a splash. Letting go of Isandro's hand, she twisted around and saw the jacket that had been draped over her shoulders floating on the water.

'Oh, God!' On an adrenaline high still, she moved quickly without thinking and almost reached it.

An arm like a steel band around her waist hauled her back from the edge.

'What the hell are you doing, woman? Do you have some sort of death wish? I have to tell you once is my limit when it comes to fishing suicidal maniacs out of the drink.'

Zoe didn't struggle against the arms banding her. She leaned back into his big, solid, hard body, allowing herself the luxury of feeling safe. She wasn't going to drown and the twins were all right.

She was still shaking with the chill of the ice in her veins but in the shelter of his arms she was protected from the wind. The feeling of security was an illusion but as illusions went this one felt good.

'Your lovely jacket.'

Isandro rested his chin on the top of her head, closed his eyes and shook his head… Jacket!

'I have others.' The woman was in need of professional help. He shifted his stance to ease the pressure on his groin and thought, *Dios*, she is not the only one!

CHAPTER SEVEN

HER LIPS TWITCHED faintly. 'The man who has everything.'

'You read the article.'

Two weeks earlier a Sunday paper had decided to dedicate half their glossy supplement to him. *The Man with the Midas Touch* was to his mind shockingly unoriginal and a perfect example of the dumbing-down of the press…ten pages that said nothing new.

He had everything? He supposed he did. But to Isandro his wealth represented not luxury or self-indulgence but the freedom to live his life just as he wanted. Did that make him selfish? Did it make him happy…? Was anyone happy?

He shook his head. *Dios*, this was not the time for a philosophical debate. This was definitely a time for action, decisive action, and the priority was warming up Zoe before she became hypo-thermic.

It did not take him long to weigh the options. Decision-making was, as the article author had suggested, Isandro's area of expertise.

'Chloe gave me her copy,' she admitted be-tween chattering teeth. 'The entire village bought the paper. They were sold out. You're a local hero...for real now...'

'Even if you didn't need my help.'

Her lips twisted into a grimace. 'I really am grateful... Stop! You can't—!'

Isandro took no notice of her protests as he began to stride up the path from the river.

'I can walk! Put me down...please put me down.'

He flashed her a look. 'You won't jump back in the river?'

'Don't be stupid.'

'Seriously, though, you're chilled through. You need to dry off and warm up.'

'I need to see the twins.'

'You think that's a good idea, looking this way?

You'll scare the life out of them,' he predicted. 'Which in Georgie's case might not be such a bad thing. But seeing you like that is likely to give Harry nightmares for a month.' He arched a brow. 'What, no "you know nothing about children, so butt out"?'

Zoe shook her head, biting her lower lip to stop it quivering. He had summed up the twins pretty accurately.

'You're right. It's me who knows nothing about bringing up children,' she wailed.

A hissing sound of exasperation left his lips as he hefted her a little higher with apparent ease. On another occasion when she wasn't busy contemplating her failure at parenting, Zoe might have been impressed. She was not exactly petite. 'I find it infinitely preferable when you are defensive and rude. This self-flagellation is boring.'

Finding herself unexpectedly placed on her feet, Zoe waited a moment for her head to stop spinning before she raised her swimming eyes to him, her quivering lips tightening. 'Oh, I'm so sorry I bored you.'

He smiled. 'Better,' he approved. 'Now, come on. What you need is a hot bath, a brandy—or maybe not brandy, you might kiss the concierge—and a change of clothes before you return to your niece and nephew.' Placing a hand on her elbow, he guided her past the selection of gleaming top-of-the-range cars parked in front of the hotel whose gardens went down to the river.

'Nice thought, but unless you have them in your pocket...' She tried a smile but her teeth were chattering too hard. Every squelchy footstep was uncomfortable. 'Where are you parked?'

'I'm not. Alex took the twins back to Ravenwood. I'll ring him, and he'll tell the twins we'll be back later.'

Belatedly Zoe realised his intention.

'You're kidding—no way!' She shook her head and shrugged off the guiding hand on her shoulder as she stared up at the recently restored art deco façade of the five-star hotel with a reputation that drew a lot of people to the area.

She'd often thought it would be nice to sample the food there—but not looking like this!

'Why would I be kidding?'

'You can't just walk in there looking like this.' She glanced at him and made the mental adjustment that while he could, she couldn't. Isandro's clothes might be sodden, but he had not been swimming, and even if he had, she acknowledged reluctantly, he would still have the presence to make any door open for him.

'Why not?'

'Well, I don't know what the dress code is but I'm pretty sure this isn't it.' She held her hands wide to reveal her sodden muddy clothes. 'They'll throw me out. They won't even let me walk across the hallowed threshold.' She took a step backwards, shaking her head in response to the gleam in his eyes. 'And before you suggest it, being carried won't change anything.'

Except possibly her pulse rate. She knew that later that night she was going to remember every little detail of being carried in his arms, which would have made her a disgrace to modern liberated womanhood had she not suspected that inside most modern independent women lurked a secret desire to be swept off her feet. And if a man like Isandro was doing the sweeping, she suspected that few would find the experience objectionable.

She couldn't help but wonder what it would have felt like if his motivation had not been totally practical—a scenario that would have required her not looking like a drowned rat and for him to not be her boss...

But this is the real world. And once more, as far as he's concerned, you've shown yourself to be a pain in the backside.

'I was not about to offer. The fact is you're not as light as you look, especially wet.' His grin widened in response to her indignant squeak. 'Who exactly do you think is going to stop us?'

Zoe, who felt oddly light-headed, didn't react to the question. 'Just take me home, Isandro.' She clutched her spinning head, suddenly feeling nauseous as frames of the past hour flashed before her eyes. 'I turned around and they weren't there, and I...'

Observing the blue discoloration of her beautiful lips, Isandro released a hissed imprecation from between clenched teeth before taking her chin firmly between his thumb and forefinger. He turned her face up to his. The problem was not so much her imminent collapse or her stubborn refusal to enter the hotel as his struggle to maintain the necessary level of objectivity.

'Look, adrenaline was the only thing that kept you on your feet, and it's crashed.' So had she.

'I do feel a bit...'

'You look a bit, too.' His glance drifted over the curve of her cheek, delineated by classic high cheekbones. Her perfect skin was marble pale, the only colour in her face was supplied by her eyes, which stood out as a flash of startling colour in a monochrome film.

'You didn't succeed in drowning yourself, so now you are inviting hypothermia.' The effort to conceal the concern her fragility evoked in him made Isandro's voice cold and flat. 'We need to warm you up, get you out of those wet clothes.'

The words had barely left his lips before a stream of images that Isandro could have done without flashed through his head. He was regaining his shattered control when a sly voice reminded him that skin-to-skin contact was a well-known treatment for hypothermia His control went out of the window!

Even a sub-zero body temperature was not going to save him from the spike of lust that hardened his already half-aroused body. *Madre di Dios*, he was turning into a sad adult version of some sex-starved teenager! For a man who prided himself on his self-control it was…not tolerable. The only thing that was going to restore him to sanity was spending a week in bed with Zoe Grace.

He exhaled. The first step to solving a problem was admitting it existed. This he had already done. The next step was to work out a strategy. He needed to treat this problem like any other and apply logic and cool objectivity. The problem was that where his housekeeper was concerned he struggled to think objectively, and as for logic—he'd just stolen a boat, for God's sake!

'I know what you're thinking,' Zoe said, looking at him over the soggy tissue she had produced and was now sniffing loudly into.

The prosaic action was rather touching, but not touching enough to hold his attention when the competition was the heaving contours of her breasts under the thin layer of drenched cotton through which her peaked nipples were clearly outlined.

'I rather doubt that, *querida*.' His thoughts were pretty rampant.

'You think I'm not fit to look after a cat, let alone two children,' she wailed, in full self-pity mode.

He did not respond with any comforting denials, but glanced rather pointedly at his watch.

This callous behaviour drew a hiss of annoyance from between her chattering teeth. 'So sorry—am I keeping you?' she said, wondering why she had thought for a second that her problems would do anything but bore the pants off him.

Her eyes dropped, running the length of his long legs, then making the journey back once she had reached his now muddy boots. She could see that, for some women, getting his pants off by whatever method would be considered a good result but she… Who was she kidding? Even on the brink of what felt like imminent hypothermia she could not stop lusting after him.

'Not at all. Feel free to go ahead and beat yourself up,' he encouraged. Zoe tried to bear her teeth in a snarl but she was shaking too hard and she bit her lip instead, drawing a pinprick of blood and his disturbing dark stare. 'But do you mind if we continue this conversation indoors?'

Zoe glanced at the hotel entrance. The golden light shining through the doors looked warm and inviting…and she was very cold. She lifted a hand to the hair that was plastered to her skull. His was, too, but in his case the effect was not drowned rat.

'I can't.' It was an invitation for him to contradict her, and he accepted it.

'Can and will,' he said, catching hold of her hand. 'We need a room.' On so many levels they needed a room!

'You can't walk in and book a room for a few hours,' she said, pointing out the obvious. At least it seemed obvious to her.

'Why not? People do. Oh, I see.' He laughed. 'You're afraid your reputation will be ruined if you're seen going into a hotel room with a man.'

'Of course not. And nobody is going to think that you…me…we…unless you normally have to half drown a woman before she'll have sex with you.'

'Not so far.'

Before she could interpret the odd inflection in his voice he had tightened his grip and virtually dragged her up the shallow flight of steps.

The warmth inside the hotel foyer hit her like a wall. So did the stares. It seemed to Zoe that a thousand eyes followed their progress.

But, as he predicted, nobody attempted to stop them, though it would have taken a very brave person to approach Isandro, who had adopted what she privately called his 'to hell with the lot of you' expression. His antagonism was probably aimed at her. This couldn't have been the way he had intended to spend his day, but the people who cleared a path for him weren't to know that.

It was amazing, she reflected enviously, as at her side Isandro gave every appearance of being genuinely oblivious to the stares and hushed comments that followed their progress across the lobby. But then he was probably used to people staring. And who could blame them? she thought as she directed a covert sideways look through her lashes at his stern profile, dishevelled but beautiful.

Even as someone who had previously not been totally sold on the dark brooding aura, she was willing to admit he was a fantastically good-looking man, who didn't just have the perfect face and body but also the indefinable extra factor. Confidence, sheer arrogance—whatever it was, he had it, and being extremely damp with his clothes spattered with mud and badly in need of a shave did not lessen it. The liberal sprinkling of stubble on his jaw lent an extra layer of air of danger, and did not exactly diminish his appeal.

So who could blame people for staring? she

thought, making a conscious effort to emulate some of his attitude. And promptly tripping over the sodden hem of her jeans. It would happen when one stared at a man and not where one was going!

The ripple of laughter at her near pratfall brought her chin up. Trotting now to keep up with Isandro, Zoe suddenly thought, To hell with this! and gave the person who had laughed an enquiring look, even managing to inject a little hauteur into it. The culprit looked away before she did.

Zoe smiled and looked ahead. No amount of shoulder hunching or wishful thinking was going to make her vanish so she might as well borrow some of Isandro's attitude, even if she couldn't carry it off with his style.

'May I help you, sir?' A man whose lapel badge identified him as the manager intercepted them when they were halfway across the lobby. He guided them towards the reception desk where the eager-to-please attentiveness continued.

The people behind the reception desk almost fell over themselves being helpful to the point of obsequiousness, but Isandro, who was firing off his list of requirements, didn't appear to notice. This was probably his life, she mused, giving impossible orders and having people fall over themselves to deliver.

After a few moments he turned to a shivering Zoe. He hadn't forgotten her after all. 'I'll be up presently. You go along.'

The manager reappeared holding a large blanket, which, on an approving nod from Isandro, he draped almost reverentially over Zoe's shoulders. 'Jeremy will show you the way, miss.'

Jeremy, neat in his uniform, nodded and motioned for her to precede him into the glass lift that he explained was for the exclusive use of the penthouse. Penthouse… Zoe almost laughed. She was well aware that if she hadn't been Isandro's satellite she wouldn't have got through the front door, let alone been given this VIP treatment.

In the second before the doors closed Isandro turned, zeroing in on her like radar. His smile flickered as he caught her eye and tipped his dark head.

As the door swished closed her heart was still beating fast. The moment, a mere nothing in reality, felt strangely intimate to Zoe, as if they were exchanging some private secret.

'I had a slight boating accident.' A half-smile flickered across her face as she realised that if Isandro had been there he would have been mystified and probably irritated by her need to explain herself to a hotel employee. Jeremy made a sympathetic noise but did not volunteer an opinion.

As soon as the door to the suite was closed, Zoe explored her palatial surroundings only as far as the bathroom that adjoined one of the bedrooms, conscious that she was leaving a trail of wet, muddy footprints.

The place was…well, wow! She had only seen hotel rooms like this in films. It felt like the set of an old movie, and she ought to be wearing a long slinky gown.

Instead she was wearing…ugh! She glanced down at her ruined clothes, her lip curling in distaste. As she peeled off the soggy garments she made an active choice not to look at herself in the mirror. It wasn't easy, as the room was full of them. Definitely a room for someone with no body issues, she thought, shedding her clothes with relief.

Free of her clothes, she did glance in passing at her reflection in a mirror. She saw long legs, a slightly rounded stomach… While she would have liked more inches up top and a bit more flesh to cover her prominent hipbones, Zoe was happy enough with her figure.

Would a man be so happy?

Her eyes half closed, her stomach muscles quivered faintly as she stroked a hand slowly down her flank. Would her first lover think her hips too narrow, or find her bottom too—she moved her hand over the curve and stopped. Her hand fell away. She was shocked—the man she saw in her mind as she imagined standing naked in front of her lover was Isandro!

Now that would be a tough audience!

The hollow-sounding laugh was not convincing and did not stop a wave of scalding shame heating her cold skin.

Refusing to dwell on the man who had now invaded, not just her life, but her subconscious, too, she walked briskly away from the sodden pile of clothes—leaving a widening pool of water on the mosaic-tiled floor—and past the massive bath set on a raised pedestal, copper and big enough to swim in. She would normally have loved to try out this opulent fantasy tub but at that moment she did not feel much like swimming, so instead she decided on the more practical option: the massive shower behind a glass wall.

As she stood under the warm spray, liberally applying the luxury bath products supplied by the hotel, she focused her thoughts on safer subjects. Just how much did it cost to spend a night here? Perhaps Isandro would take the cost from her pay?

'No!' Fear and anger bubbling inside her, she picked up a sponge and began to apply it roughly to her skin. Why was it that the wretched man managed to infiltrate her every thought? When she finally stopped rubbing and dropped the sponge, her skin was glowing and tingling pink, and her mind was a blissful, exfoliated blank.

Picking up the shampoo, she lathered her hair for a long time after it was squeaky clean. She stood still like an alabaster statue, her eyes closed, her face lifted to the warm spray, thinking nothing.

The nothing vanished the moment she emerged from the shower and heard sounds of activity in the sitting room. Immediately tension slid down her spine.

'For goodness' sake, Zoe, get over yourself!' she told herself impatiently. 'You fancy him. Big deal! Half the planet fancies him so what makes you so special, other than the fact he thinks you're an incompetent idiot?' She sniffed and reached for one of the gowns hanging from a hook. 'And staff. He doesn't kiss staff even when they kiss him.' That mortifying memory was going to stay with her for a long time.

She wasn't even a colleague. She was the help.

She took a deep breath as she tightened the

belt on her robe and flicked her wet hair back from her face.

As she entered the sitting room cautiously it was immediately clear there had been considerable activity in her absence. The table beside the open doors that led to the Juliet balcony had been laid with silver cutlery and fancily folded Irish linen napkins, and the antique candelabra in the middle was lit. It looked like a classic stage set for seduction… She could only assume that the staff had got the wrong idea.

She didn't immediately see Isandro, who had been sitting on a leather chesterfield in an alcove. She was alerted by the creak of leather before his throaty drawl.

'Feeling better?'

She flinched and spun around just as he got to his feet. Her skin had tingled when she'd ruthlessly scrubbed it, but now the tingle went deeper… I was better, but I'm not any more, she thought as she pasted on a polite smile.

'Yes, thank you. That smells good.' She nodded towards the domed covered serving dish set on the console table before looking at him—or, rather, past him.

'Clothes maketh the man' was not a phrase that applied to Isandro. He looked good in clothes, but he looked equally good, actually much better, without them…well, almost without them. He was wearing a robe similar to her own but on him the superior hotel-issue garment reached his thigh and revealed more of his dark hair-roughened skin than she was comfortable with.

'I almost came to look for you.'

It had taken all his willpower and the seemingly constant flow of waiters through the place not to follow the sound of the running water and his own instincts.

His own shower had been ice cold, which had given him a temporary partial relief from his agony, but the moment she'd walked into the room with a freshly scrubbed face and nothing more than an ankle on show he had been painfully aroused and unable to think about anything but throwing her on the bed. His desire had no subtlety; it was sheer primal hunger.

He wanted her so badly he could taste it.

'I only need rescuing once a day.' Her lips formed a smile but her eyes conspicuously avoided making contact with his. Isandro could feel her tension from where he stood. 'Did you contact Alex?' she asked, as businesslike as someone could be when bare-faced and barefoot. She ran her tongue across her dry lips. She didn't even have any lipstick to hide behind, though it was doubtful if a slash of cherry red would have made her feel more confident.

'Yes, he's got Rowena to come over and baby-sit.'

'Rowena.' Zoe gave a sigh of relief, losing some of her stiff formality as she smiled. 'Thank you.'

Isandro's eyes travelled up from her bare feet to the top of her wet head. The section in between was covered in a thick layer of fluffy white bath-robe, but the suggestion of curves, the thought of the soft skin it hid, sent his imagination into overdrive.

'What can I get you?' He walked over to the table and lifted a lid on one of the dishes.

You on a sandwich, she thought, but bit her lip. 'Thanks, but I can't eat. I should get back.' Before I make a total fool of myself.

'Why?' He looked irritated by her response. 'The twins are being well cared for. Or don't you think Rowena can cope?'

'It's not a matter of her coping.' Rowena was totally capable. The young woman's parents had been good friends of Dan and Laura, and the twins loved their daughter, who ran the local stables. 'I don't want to take advantage.'

Her sister and brother-in-law had had a lot of friends and it was good to know that in an emergency they were there. But it was important to her to stand on her own feet and not become reliant. Or infatuated, she thought, looking directly at him for the first time.

He arched a strongly delineated ebony brow. Everything about his face was strong. 'Have you ever said no when someone asks a favour? No, you haven't. But when they want to return the favour it becomes "taking advantage"?'

The mockery in his voice as he adopted a very

shaky falsetto to mimic her brought a lump to Zoe's throat.

'I'm glad I give you something to laugh about.'

'I'm not laughing. I admire independence but not when it becomes bloody-minded stubbornness.' Sometimes he wondered when she slept, or if. His critical glance moved to the violet smudges beneath her spectacular eyes. She was struggling to fit into a job she was unsuited for, and struggling to be the perfect parent. It was admirable but impossible. Why couldn't the woman embrace her imperfections? He had!

The insight sent a stab of shock through Isandro. She roused feelings that he flatly refused to recognise as protective tenderness. He refused because he associated the emotions with weakness. It made him angry. *She* made him angry!

'What are you trying to prove, Zoe?' he asked, his voice hard.

'I'm not trying to prove anything!'

Glaring, her eyes slid down his body as he sat down and leaned back on the leather sofa. Stretching his long legs out, he folded one ankle across the other. The hair-roughened skin of his muscular calves looked very dark against the white of the hotel robes. She was wearing nothing underneath. Was he...?

Shivering, she stopped the speculation from progressing into dangerous territory and dragged her gaze back to his face.

'In that case take five minutes off from being a martyr and give us all a break.'

She sucked in a gulping breath, embracing the rush of anger as she clenched her fists. 'There's nobody here but you and me.'

'Exactly, and I won't tell if you fall off your perfect parent pedestal. Just you and me...what could be cosier?'

The question drew a gurgle from her throat. 'Oh, I don't know—how about hang gliding over an active volcano?'

And there was something combustible about him, even when he was still and silent like now, his long, lean body relaxed. She had the impression that he could explode into action at any moment.

He let out a low chuckle, his expression sobering as he added, 'Are you planning to put your life on hold for the next ten or fifteen years?'

'Fifteen years!' She snorted. 'I'm not thinking any farther ahead than next month's bills.' She found his anger inexplicable. 'I'm a single parent. My priority has to be the twins.'

'Single parents have been known to have sex.'

CHAPTER EIGHT

ZOE BLINKED, THE COLOUR flying to her cheeks as she lost any fragile illusion of composure. 'Since when were we talking about sex?'

'It's part of a healthy, well-balanced life. We're always talking about sex, even when we're talking about the weather. It's the subtext.'

She flushed and snapped in protest, 'I was drunk when that happened before.'

'You're not drunk now.' So there was zero reason for gentlemanly behaviour. 'And I'm not a teenager. I'm tired of the game.' And the frustration was killing him.

He had come up with a workable solution. Now all he had to do was sell it. Isandro did not doubt his ability to do so. That was what he was good at: selling ideas; producing packages that made everyone think they had a good deal.

Zoe had anticipated his anger. After all, from

his point of view she was a grade A nuisance. But she had not imagined this level of simmering fury. Even while he had been yelling at her over capsizing the boat, there had been an underlying gentleness, almost a tenderness, in his manner.

Searching his lean, handsome face now Zoe could see no trace of the tenderness. The gleam in his deep-set dark eyes was hard and calculating... She shivered.

'I don't play games,' she protested. 'And I happen to think that someone who changes his girlfriends like socks and never sees them during daylight hours is not qualified to preach to me on what constitutes a healthy, well-balanced life!'

Having said her piece, she sat down with a bump on the sofa opposite him, her cheeks burning. She drew the folds of the robe around her like a tent and pulled her knees up to her chest.

'Obviously, how you live your life is none of my business, but that goes both ways. I work for you, but that doesn't give you a right to criticise my lifestyle unless it impinges on my ability to do my work.'

'Pardon me for stepping over the line,' he drawled, tipping his head in mock apology. 'But I think that line has been blurred from day one with us.'

Eyes trained on the gaping neckline of her robe and the exposed curve of one smooth shoulder, he exhaled through flared nostrils, combating the stab of lust by focusing on the disruption this woman had caused in his life, and not the fact he wanted to touch her skin.

This situation was of his own making. He had broken a fundamental rule. He had allowed the lines to become blurred, and he needed a strict demarcation between his personal and professional lives.

Her eyes lowered. 'I know I made a bad first impression, but I hoped that by now you'd see that I really am capable of—'

'Drowning yourself?' An image of her vanishing under the water began to play on a loop in his head, the images accompanied by the dull bass soundtrack of his blood pumping in his ears.

She flashed him a reproachful look. 'No. Being a good housekeeper.'

He laughed, and it sounded cruel to Zoe, who sat hunched watching him. 'You're a terrible housekeeper.'

A part of her despised wanting to cry. She held the tears back by sniffing and concentrating on the part of her that wanted to throw something at him.

'I've made a few mistakes,' she conceded.

His brows hit his hairline. 'A few! You can't give the most basic instruction, you fall for any sob story and you invite people to take advantage of you.'

'I think more of people than you do. I trust them.'

'I know—that's why you're sacked.'

He hadn't intended to deliver the news quite so brutally, but a combination of need and frustration bypassed his subtlety circuits. And diplomacy did not come easy when you had a slow-motion nightmare playing on a loop in your head. He prided himself on his ability to apply cool logic to all situations, but for a moment back there on the water, even though he'd known the boat would get him to her quicker, he had been within a whisper of following his instincts and diving in.

If he had, who knew what the outcome might have been? She called herself a strong swimmer but he knew what he had seen. Though he actually was a strong swimmer, there remained a question mark—could he have reached her in time?

It was possible they might both have perished.

She stiffened as she shot to her feet, every muscle in her body clenched and defensive, refusing to acknowledge the cold fear in her belly. Clasping her hands together, she blew out her breath slowly and flicked back her wet hair.

'What did you say?' Her tone was conversational. She had obviously misheard him—nobody would be that brutal, that totally...totally vile.

'You're sacked.'

Desperation overcame her anger and she crumbled. 'I'm really trying—'

'Do not beg, Zoe. This is not open for discussion.'

She bit her lip.

'It doesn't matter how much you try. You're uniquely unsuited to the role of housekeeper. I think it'll be easier all around if we cut our losses rather than drag this out. You are not the sort of housekeeper I need.' You're the sort of sex I need.

Panic made her voice shrill as she came back, 'I could be. It's just I can't relax around you...' She caught his look and added quickly, 'Because you're my employer.'

Quite suddenly he was tired of this pretence. Sensual mouth compressed, his chiselled cheekbones jutting hard against his golden skin, he silenced her with a sharp jerk of his head as he rose to his feet. 'That situation has got nothing to do with the fact I pay your wages. A strong sexual connection makes all our encounters less than relaxing, especially when you work so hard trying to pretend it doesn't exist.'

Zoe turned her head, her mouth open to produce a strong rebuttal, her eyes connected with his glowing dark gaze. Her biggest fear had been him guessing the way she felt, and now he had. So what, she thought despairingly, was the point denying it?

'Don't you find it exhausting, Zoe?' he asked softly.

She stood there mutely staring at him. Inside she was dying of sheer mortification. This was her boss saying he knew she secretly lusted after him. What was she meant to say to that?

For a split second his resolve wavered. She looked so pale, so vulnerable. But it only wavered briefly. Another month like this one and he'd be a basket case.

'I can only assume you've had some problems in the past with female staff and…crushes, but I promise you're safe from me.'

He didn't want to be safe from her.

'Good to know, but you're still sacked.'

She flinched. The bastard had said it the way someone remarked on the weather. Somewhere deep inside her, rage stirred. 'Because I don't fancy you.'

'If that were true, there would be no problem.'

Her chest swelled as she flung him a look of withering contempt. 'Even if you were right I have my own rules, too. And the first one is that I never have sex with a man I don't respect. Believe you me, that rules you out, you contemptuous little snake!'

He gave a low throaty chuckle.

'Why didn't you just sack me on that first day?' That would have been bad but this was worse. Thinking her job was secure, she'd allowed herself to relax, she'd allowed herself to sit here thinking stupid ridiculous thoughts about him, imagining that they might even... Stupid...stupid...stupid! She was so angry with herself she wanted to scream. She took a deep breath and slung a look of loathing his way.

'I didn't sack you at that point because my company is in the middle of some sensitive negotiations which could mean a lot of...' He made a dismissive gesture with his hand. 'You are not interested in the whys, but the success of this deal will mean something in the region of a thousand jobs over a five-year period.'

'What's that got to do with me?'

'It's about protecting my company's brand. Any negative publicity would send the clients running for the hills, and the story of me sacking a woman because she used my property to host a charity fund-raiser would be the worst-possible PR.'

Trying to think beyond the static buzz in her head, a combination of anger and panic, she only really processed one word in two of what he was saying. 'I don't know what you're talking about.'

'Because you are an innocent.'

How long would her savings last…a month, two…? After that what was she going to do?

'I really hate you.' Her snarl was shaky but filled with venom and her eyes gleamed with loathing as she glared up at him. She grabbed at a side table, afraid that her shaking knees were about to give way. This body blow on top of the events of that afternoon had taken a physical as well as mental toll.

'Calm down. There's no need to react this way. It's not as though you enjoy the job.'

Calm down? What planet did this man live on?

'We can't all do jobs we enjoy. Some of us do jobs because we need to survive.' This job had been her plan A, and she didn't have a plan B. She wiped her brow as she felt the panic crowding in on her again.

'Will you stop acting as though you're a heroine in a Victorian melodrama and I'm the villain?'

She flashed him a look of sheer incredulity and shook her head. He made it sound as though she was overreacting. 'If the black hat fits…?'

With an exaggerated roll of his eyes he placed his hands on her shoulders, exerting enough pressure to force her back down onto the sofa. 'If you'd stop for a minute and let me explain. I'm not throwing you out anywhere. I'm suggesting that you move to the end of the drive, that's all.'

'What are you talking about?'

'The gatehouse.' The solution had been staring him in the face all along! Now that he had had his eureka moment, he couldn't understand why he hadn't thought about it earlier.

'The one you've just decorated?'

The building in question had not been included in the initial refurbishment of the estate because there had apparently been some planning dispute over a proposed extension, but this had recently been resolved. Zoe had not been involved with the renovation but the builders had packed up and left a couple of weeks ago and the team of decorators had literally finished the previous day.

'If I'm not working for you how can—?'

'I'm suggesting you and the children move into the gatehouse, pay a nominal rent...'

'With what?' No job meant no money, which meant... Oh, God, she couldn't think what it meant. She was no longer in a position to sleep on a friend's couch until she sorted things. The twins needed a home and stability—they needed a guardian who didn't go around losing her job!

I am such a loser.

Well, if she was a loser, he was a total bastard!

'I have a friend who has bought an art gallery.

She is looking for someone to front it. I have spoken to her about you...'

Polly's astonished response when he had explained that his unsuitable housekeeper's domestic situation meant he couldn't simply let her go without providing some sort of safety net was still fresh in his mind.

'Since when did you worry about dismissing someone who wasn't up to the job, Isandro? And why are you going to so much trouble to help find the girl a job?'

She had accepted his explanation without question.

'So this is about avoiding bad PR. What a relief. For a moment there—' she laughed '—I thought you'd become a bleeding heart!'

'She is happy to offer you a trial,' Isandro told Zoe.

'What makes you think I'd be any less terrible at running an art gallery than I am running a house?' Zoe asked bitterly.

'You are artistic.'

'How would you know?'

'Had you not been accepted on a fine arts degree course before your sister and her husband died?'

In the middle of a miserable sniff, Zoe lifted her incredulous glance to his face. 'How did you know that?'

He shrugged and dropped his gaze. 'Tom might have mentioned it.'

'But why would your friend give me this job?'

'I asked her.'

'A permanent job?'

'Very few things in life are permanent, but there would be a very good severance package,' he told her smoothly. 'Enough for you to pay your way through art college as you planned and employ childcare in the meantime. I understand they run an excellent foundation fine arts course on an evening basis at the local college.'

'I don't understand. Why would this woman pay me a—' her nose wrinkled; what had he called it? '—severance package?'

'She wouldn't.'

Zoe shook her head as the confusion deepened.

'I would.'

'But I wouldn't be working for you.'

'Not as such,' he conceded. 'The point is, Zoe, the attraction is not one-sided. I want you in my bed and I am a man in a position to make my fantasies come true. You are my fantasy, Zoe.'

Things fell into place in her head with an almost audible clunk. She shot to her feet—no longer shaking, no longer terrified, just furious.

'Let me get this straight. This job you're talking about, it's as…your mistress?'

He shrugged. 'That's an old-fashioned term.'

She stuck out her chin, her blue eyes sparkling with wrathful contempt. 'I'm an old-fashioned girl.' He had no idea how old-fashioned. 'Though I suppose you think I should be flattered. Isn't it a bit of a risk, though? We've never even slept together. How would you know that I'd be…any good in the bedroom?'

'It takes two, and I think when a woman literally shakes with lust when I look at her I'm willing to take the risk on a sight-unseen basis—'

'My God!' she gasped. 'You really think I'm

shallow enough to want to sleep with a man who is obviously deeply in love with himself. A man whose only redeeming feature as far as I can tell is a pretty face and a moderately all right body.'

Fingers crossed, because that was a lie. He had the body of an Adonis. She gave a derisive sniff and arched a brow before laughing.

'Yes, I do.' His sloe-dark eyes drifted over her lush sinuous curves shrouded beneath the robe, and his mouth grew dry at the thought of slipping the loose knot of the belt looped around her narrow waist.

It was an uphill struggle to act as though his slow, sexy smile was doing nothing to her. She knew that sex appeal wasn't just about looks, but the idea that she was any man's erotic fantasy—let alone a man like Isandro—was shocking. She swallowed and pressed both hands to her stomach, shamefully aware that the deep quivers that rippled low in her pelvis were not caused by shock. What he was suggesting was wrong on more levels than she could count, it went against every principle she held dear, yet she was excited… What does that say about me?

'Besides, we don't have to wait. This is the perfect opportunity to find out if it's as good as I think it will be.' The sweep of his hand took in the big bed piled with cushions, the open French door against which the light curtains fluttered in the breeze.

In the distance Zoe could hear a flock of geese landing on the water. She went hot, cold, then hot again.

'I'm not selling my body.'

'That's good, because I've never paid for sex.'

'What do you call what you're suggesting?'

'I'm suggesting we remove the barrier that is preventing us both doing what we want to. If you are no longer on my payroll we can be equal.'

'I'll never be equal to you. I'll always be superior!'

'Bravo!' he drawled.

Her lips tightened. 'Don't you dare patronise me! And why make up that stupid story about your friend?'

'That is not invented. It is real. I do have a friend who owns a gallery.'

Zoe felt a stab of something she didn't immediately recognise as jealousy. 'A female friend?'

Could you sound more jealous if you tried?

'Her name is Polly Warrender. She inherited a theatre from her husband.' Zoe had heard of the Warrender theatre, but then pretty much everyone had. 'When she diversified and bought into an art gallery she came to me for advice.'

She stifled a theatrical yawn, but the gesture unwittingly drew his eyes to the soft full curve of her rosy lips. 'So, let me guess, she listened to you and made a fortune,' she inserted with a roll of her eyes.

'Actually she ignored my advice and bought it and, yes, made a fortune.' He gave a faint smile. 'A smallish one.'

'So you were wrong?'

He reached out and tangled a wet curl around one long brown finger and drawled, 'You've discovered the chink in my infallible armour. Please do me a favour and keep it to yourself.'

As he released the curl his finger brushed her cheek. It barely made contact, but Zoe, who had been holding her breath, felt an electric tingle pass through her body all the way to her curling toes.

His voice was a soft attractive buzz. She could hear what he was saying, but over and above the words was a louder buzz—a combination of her own heartbeat and the thrum of the deep hunger that was coursing through her veins with each beat of her heart as she stared at the deep V of golden chest dark against the white towelling.

It took every ounce of her self-control to stop herself reaching out and touching him... She curled her hands into fists and tucked them behind her back.

'I put her onto the decommissioned church that was up for sale in town as a possible site for a new gallery. She has wanted to expand into this area for some time, so she owes me a favour. She is genuinely looking for someone to run it, and you have an art background... So it is perfectly feasible for you to live here and commute to do the foundation course.'

'And amuse you in bed.' He acknowledged her bitter addition with a tilt of his head. 'You have it all worked out.'

He gave a smile. 'The secret of success is taking control of events and not allowing them to control you.'

Yeah, you carry on telling yourself that, Isandro, if it makes you feel any better. The fact was he had felt out of control since the moment he had met this woman. From day one she had managed to turn his well-ordered life into chaos.

She shook her head. 'Don't you dare smile. I'm not listening to a word you're saying.'

He took the hands she had pressed to her ears and pressed them against his chest. Then holding her eyes with his, he brushed his lips across her cheek.

'You're not shouting, though,' he murmured against her mouth.

She wasn't. Zoe was barely breathing. Her body felt strange and tingly, as though it didn't belong to her. Her arms and legs felt heavy as though a great weight were dragging her down. Dizzy, she clutched at the towelling of his robe. Somehow it parted and her hands were flat on his skin, the warmth seeping into her cold fingers, the heavy thud of his heartbeat mingling with the frantic clamour of her riotous pulse.

Common sense told her to push him away.

'This isn't going to happen.' Why was she whispering? She should be shouting.

'If you say so, *querida*.' His big hand sank into her wet hair, cupping the back of her skull. His long fingers tangled in her hair while his thumb trailed tingling paths down her cheek. His breath was coming fast and hot against her neck.

Her knees gave out, but before she could slide to the floor his arms snaked around her waist. He was so close that his face was a dark blur. She could see the predatory glow of his beautiful eyes. Her own eyes burned but she couldn't blink, she couldn't look away, not until he tugged at the soft pink flesh of her lower lip, holding it between his teeth. Then her eyes squeezed tight closed as she released a soft sibilant sigh and opened her palms flat on his chest, pushing them under the thick fabric of the robe, up over his warm skin to his shoulders.

Still she didn't push. Like someone in a dream she clung, and still he didn't kiss her. The scent of his warm male body in her nostrils, she was desperate for the taste of him. The need consumed her utterly, so strong that it blotted every other thought from her mind. He radiated raw power, and it excited her unbearably, sent a primitive heat sweeping through her in waves crashing over her. She felt herself going under.

Need, primitive need, raw and all-consuming, blinding lust controlled his actions as he tilted her face up. *Dios*, but he had wanted to kiss her for… It felt like a lifetime.

His tongue slid between her parted lips and Zoe's brain closed down as instinct took over. Her moan was lost in the warm recesses of his mouth as her lips parted to deepen the sensual invasion.

She kissed him back, greedily drinking in the

taste of him, wanting more…wanting everything. He hauled her body into him. His hands slipped down to her bottom as, cupping it, he lifted her off the ground. Without thinking, she wrapped her long legs tight around his waist as she framed his face between her hands, gave a throaty sigh and whispered, 'God, but you are so beautiful… the most beautiful man.'

With a deep groan that rose up in his throat he plundered Zoe's mouth, kissing her with barely controlled desperation, stealing the breath from her lungs, lighting a passion that flared into violent life. As she kissed him back with a wild and unrestrained hunger, satisfying the mutual need between them, everything else ceased to exist.

Her fingers dug into the muscles of his shoulders, her legs tightening around his waist as she fought to get closer to him, her strength fuelled by the primal desire to be joined with him…be one.

Joined with her that way still, he walked blindly towards the bed.

Zoe felt as if she were falling—and then she

was really falling and he was falling on top of her. A pillow beneath her head, she barely noticed the weight of his body on top of her until he levered himself off.

Panting, her eyes as dark as midnight, she gave a small cry of protest, then she saw what he was doing. Kneeling over her, Isandro was shrugging off his robe.

'Oh, my God!'

He was long and lean, his skin gleaming like burnished gold. Not an ounce of excess flesh blurred the perfect lines of his powerful body. Every bone and sinew of him was perfect, like a bronzed statue. A rampantly, fully aroused bronzed statue.

She bit down hard on her full lower lip as heat washed her skin with a warm rosy flush. Her initial shock at the earthy image was replaced by a stomach-clenching, incapacitating, lustful longing that closed down every logic circuit in her brain.

His grin was fierce and his laughter strained as

he husked, 'If you look at me like that, *querida*, this thing is going to be over before it has begun.'

'I want you,' she whispered, pulling herself up onto her knees. 'So badly…' She reached out and touched him, unable to believe her daring as she curled her fingers around the shaft of his erection. Silky smooth and rock hard, he pulsed hotly against her small hand. 'You feel—' her breasts quivered as she gave a fractured sigh and continued to stare, fascinated, at him '—incredible.'

A hiss left his lips as he caught her wrist.

'Too much,' he muttered, pressing her body back onto the bed before he joined her. Arranging his long lean length beside her, he kissed her, a kiss full of passion and promise that made words redundant. Lifting his head, he stroked her face and held her eyes as he reached for the tie on her robe.

The embarrassment she had anticipated did not materialise but the voluptuous pleasure did as he whispered fiercely, 'You are exquisite, flawless.'

His searing gaze swept upwards slowly, greedily drinking her in as it took in every detail from her narrow feet and ankles, the long elegant length of her legs, and over her belly. Then finally to her lovely, pertly pointed breasts.

His hand came to cover one perfect soft mound. Her skin was flawless. He could smell the perfume of the soap on her skin, and the faint but distinctive delicate, musky scent of her arousal made his vision mist red.

As he massaged the smooth skin, his touch firm but sensitive, running his thumb with slow deliberate strokes across the sensitised peaks, Zoe gasped and muttered his name. Her head thrashed wildly back and forth on the pillow. The pleasure was so intense—beyond words, she clenched her hands into fists at her sides as she felt herself losing her struggle to stay in control.

Then his mouth was on her breasts, his hands on her body, touching her awakening senses. With a soft sigh of surrender, she stopped trying and gave herself up to the desire flowing like warm wine through her veins. She almost felt like laughing with the sense of release. Who knew that losing control, feeling enough trust to give it over to someone else, could feel like this?

She reached for him, her fingers tangling in his dark hair, holding him against her as she stroked the skin of his muscled shoulders. The raw power in him, the dramatic contrasts of his hard angularity and her own softness, her roundness, was more exciting than she could have dreamed possible.

Isandro lifted his head and smiled at her with his glorious eyes, a dark fierce smile filled with promise, then he kissed her belly, drawing a hoarse gasp from Zoe, and ran his tongue over the quivering skin, drawing a line that terminated just above the apex of her thighs.

At the first touch of his hands between her legs need exploded through her. She loosed a keening cry as her hips lifted off the bed. Her entire body ached and trembled with desire; her mouth opened but she had no words, just his name, which she said over and over. And when she stopped he lifted his head and said, 'Again, say it again.'

She did, and at the same time opened her legs in mute invitation, inviting skilful touch of his fingers over the slick, moist, swollen folds of her femininity, and the tight, sensitive nub they protected.

The first skin-to-skin contact was electric. Then, as her arched spine made contact with the bed and he pressed down on top of her, it was totally, utterly blissful, a cocktail of intoxicating physical sensations that made her senses spiral and spin. Bright lights exploded behind her eyelids as she closed her eyes.

Her hips moved in a grinding motion as she rubbed herself against his erection as it dug into her thigh, then her soft belly. The pressure building inside her made her thrash around, bite his neck as she dragged her fingers down his back, clutching at the firm contours of his tight, muscular buttocks.

Unable to bear the erotic friction of his erection against her any longer, she grabbed his hair, drawing his face to hers, and kissing him hard, whispered, 'Please!'

With a savage smile he held her eyes as he drove deep into her body. The breath left her in a shocked gasp that was drowned out by his deep growl of pleasure. Her heart racing, her eyes closed tight, she concentrated on the intense pleasure of each slow, measured movement of his hips as he moved inside her body. There was layer after layer of sensations that she had never imagined she could feel.

Each thrust built the erotic pleasure that she encouraged with each sinuous, sensuous grind of her hips responding to age-old instincts she was delighted to discover.

When the climax hit her, she was unprepared for the strength of the expanding wave of pleasure and her eyes flew wide with shock.

'Perfect, just go with it, my clever, beautiful…' His eyes held her while she rode the wave. He waited until she reached the vortex of the storm before he allowed himself to find his own release and thrust one final time into her.

When Zoe floated back to earth, she was curled

up in his arms, her head resting against his thudding heart, her sweat-slick limbs tangled with his.

'Well, I never saw that one coming. I remember hearing you say you did not approve of casual sex but I never equated that with… Was there a bad experience that put you off sex I should have known about?'

It seemed the only explanation for how a woman as sexy and passionate as Zoe Grace could be a virgin. And her surrender had been total; she had held nothing back. He had sensed the passion beneath the surface, but what he had released had startled and delighted him almost as much as the discovery she was a virgin.

'No bad experience, I just… I've moved around a lot and never got time to make any sort of lasting relationship. Not that this is lasting…obviously.' There was a short awkward pause. Dear God, it was a strange world when she was embarrassed to admit that, a secret romantic, she had always felt uneasy about casual sex.

'You must have had boyfriends.'

'Of course I have—I'm not a freak. I had boy-friends but they all seemed to suggest I was not very…good at that sort of stuff.' Her last date had culminated in a nasty little scene when the man who invited her to dinner had accused her of being a tease when she could not agree that the correct payment for a dinner was a make-out session in the back seat of a car.

He gave a throaty laugh of incredulity. 'I think you have been keeping the wrong company.'

She twisted in his arms and flipped onto her stomach, resting her chin on her elbows and affording him an excellent view of her breasts. 'And you're the right company?' she challenged.

He was definitely the right lover.

'It felt pretty right to me.'

'So what happens now?'

His wicked grin flashed. 'Give me five minutes.'

'I mean after this?' Had he really been serious about moving her and the twins into the gatehouse?

CHAPTER NINE

'I THOUGHT I had already made that clear.'

'But after?' Isandro was hot for her now, but Zoe did not anticipate the situation would last and when he lost interest, what then? 'When I am no longer flavour of the day?'

'That moment,' he purred, stroking the silky smooth skin of her forearm, 'feels like a long way off.'

'But it might not be.'

'Well, that is catered for. You will continue to live in the gatehouse for as long as it pleases you. It seems to me a win, win situation.'

He could say that but he wasn't on the brink of falling in love. Who was she kidding? Zoe thought bleakly. She was already in love and had been for the past weeks. She was going to be devastated when this was over, but she was going to be devastated anyway so why not have some weeks of delicious mind-blowing sex with this gorgeous man to remember and some financial security for the twins?

'All right, but no.' She twisted away from the hand that reached for her, knowing that once he touched her she wouldn't be able to think straight, let alone consider consequences. 'There have to be some rules.'

Isandro stared at her, taken aback—he made the rules.

'I don't want this to affect the twins. I don't want them to know about us. We have to be discreet. We know this is just sex but they are just...' Whichever way she looked, there were aspects to this arrangement that didn't feel right.

He tipped his head. 'That seems fair.' He tangled his fingers in her hair and kissed her mouth. 'Do not look so worried. We have weeks of pleasure ahead of us. You are not some little girl seeking the attention of men and mistaking it for love. This is an equal relationship of two people who know what they want.'

'What do you want?'

'You, *querida*, you in so many ways.'

She shivered. 'Many ways?'

His smile made her heart flip. 'Come here and let me show you.'

Zoe and the twins had been established in the gatehouse for six weeks. Her passion with Isandro had not flagged, and six weeks was new ground for him. Abiding by rules set by someone else was also new and on occasion frustrating.

There came a tapping on the window of his study—which had recently been knocked through to make room for the extra office equipment he needed since he had made the decision to do more work from home.

Isandro looked up from the computer screen.

When the red-headed figure at the window saw him she began to gesticulate wildly. A second later she vanished, and there was a clattering sound.

With a sigh Isandro levered himself up from his chair, stretching the kinks from his spine as he walked towards the window. Pulling up the sash, he leaned out. Georgina was lying beside an overturned crate she had presumably dragged over to the window and fallen off. She was picking herself up.

'What are you doing?'

'Looking for you, obviously.' Ever irrepressible, she dusted off the seat of her jeans.

'Did you hurt yourself?'

The kid treated the question with the scorn she appeared to think it deserved, shaking her head and looking offended by the question.

Like aunt, like niece, he thought.

'I would have gone to Chloe but they're not back until tomorrow. I can't wait to see Hannah again and she's walking with crutches, and there isn't really anyone else.'

So not first choice, or even second. 'I feel honoured.'

'If Zoe died, would we get put in a home?'

His half-sardonic smile snuffed like a candle caught in a chill draft and Isandro did suddenly feel as though a cold fist had plunged deep into his belly.

'Zoe is not going to die.'

'No...?' Her niece sounded scarily uncertain.

'What has happened to your aunt Zoe?' he asked, ruthlessly reining in his imagination and struggling to keep his tone light.

'She says she's fine but she doesn't look fine and she—'

He held up a hand. 'Wait there. I will be with you momentarily.'

Snatching up his jacket on the way out, he paused only to close his laptop before leaving the house. Outside Georgie was trotting around the side of the house to meet him when he emerged.

'Zoe sent you?'

She shook her head. 'She'll be mad with me,' she predicted gloomily.

'She doesn't need to know that you came to get me.'

Her eyes flew wide with shock. 'That would be lying!' Children were a minefield.

'Of course it would, and of course you should never lie...especially to your aunt.'

The child looked unconvinced as she climbed into the passenger seat of his car.

'Now tell me what is wrong.'

When they arrived at the lodge they entered through her open back door where Harry, his face scrunched in concentration, was standing on a kitchen chair trying to open a tin with an opener that looked like an antique. His small fingers looked perilously near the razor-sharp edges.

Conscious it might not be a good idea to startle him, Isandro walked across and, after a friendly pat on the shoulder, extricated the tin from his grip.

'Let me—there's a knack to this. There you go.' He glanced at the label. 'Chicken soup.'

'Mum always gave us chicken soup when we were sick. I thought I'd make Zoe some.'

'Good idea, but let's wait until we see if she wants to eat just now.'

'Until she stops throwing up, stupid,' his sister inserted critically.

'I'm not stupid.'

Isandro cleared his throat. 'How about if you two go?' Two expectant faces turned to him. 'Go to the shop and get me some...' He paused. 'Are you allowed to walk to the shop?'

They both shook their heads.

'Right, well...' *Madre di Dios*, give me a room of CEOs any day of the week.

'We could clean out your car. It was very messy. For money,' Georgie offered.

Her brother cast her a sideways warning look. 'For free.'

His sister sighed heavily.

'That would be very helpful.' His car had been valet cleaned the previous week. 'I will go and see how your aunt is feeling, but don't worry. It sounds like she has the flu bug that is doing the rounds.' He moved towards the hallway.

'Are you Zoe's boyfriend?'

Isandro might not be good with children but he did not fall into that trap. He paused and turned. His amused expression was not a direct denial but he hoped they took it as such. 'Is that why you came to get me? Because you think I am her boyfriend?'

'No, we came to get you because she was saying your name in the night. She woke us up and when we went in she was awake but really hot.'

'I told you it was just a nightmare,' Harry said.

A woman's nightmare…children certainly had a way of keeping a man's ego in check.

Isandro made his way to the bedroom at the front of the cottage. The door was ajar, and he pushed it open and found the curtains in the airy room pulled shut. The light filtering through the striped fabric illuminated the figure in the bed lying with one arm curled around her head.

He was used to feeling the tug of sexual attraction when he looked at her, used to feeling the electrical tingle when she was close. As he stared at her now, looking both vulnerable and utterly desirable—they were both there but there was something else in the mix, something he struggled to define as he stood nailed to the spot while something imploded in his skull.

Then she moved and shifted, groaning softly

before she licked her lips as her eyelashes fluttered against her cheek. 'Harry.'

'Not Harry.'

The eyelashes parted to reveal blue blurry eyes. 'Oh, God,' she groaned. 'What are you doing here?'

He had had more enthusiastic welcomes. 'How are you feeling?'

She raised herself groggily up on one elbow, causing the nightdress she wore to slip over one shoulder. He felt a stab of inappropriate lust.

'Fine,' she croaked.

'I admire the stiff upper lip, naturally, but an honest answer would be more helpful.'

Zoe turned her head on the pillow and aimed a look of simmering dislike on him. He wanted to know what she felt like? Fine, she'd tell him.

'I feel like death warmed up. Happy?' She lowered herself with a groan onto the pillow. 'And I suppose I look that way, too.'

'Pretty bad,' he agreed, his mocking smile vanishing as her lips began to tremble. 'Are you crying?'

'Oh, well, so sorry I couldn't manage to put on my make-up for your benefit, but nobody asked you here.' Her brow furrowed. 'What are you doing here anyway?'

'Georgie came to get me.'

'Oh, God, she shouldn't have.'

'They are worried.'

Zoe clapped a hand to her aching head and groaned. 'I told them I'm fine. It's just a bug or something.'

'Symptom-wise, could you be a little more precise?'

'If I tell you will you go away? I have cymbals playing in my head, I ache all over and I feel sick...' She gave a him a narrow-eyed glare of 'Is that precise enough for you?'

'Very succinct. I am assuming our date tonight is off.'

Zoe didn't have the energy to prise her eyelids apart but she found the strength to correct him.

'We don't have a date. It's just sex. Do I know it's just sex? he asks me, like I'm a total idiot,' she mumbled. The comment he had made in the aftermath of the frantic love-making session they had fitted in while the children were having their riding lesson had been playing in her head all through the long interminable night.

'So how is our patient?'

This time Zoe's eyes didn't open as she resisted the temptation to declare she was nobody's patient.

'Doctor, who sent for you?' He had to have heard what she'd said. She comforted herself with the thought that doctors, like priests, couldn't blab about their patients. Presumably the Montero name, or possibly the cheque book, had made the man forget that GPs no longer made house calls at the weekend, she brooded, with a cynical sniff that became a cough.

Neither man answered her question.

'Beyond the general crankiness, she has a headache, joint pain and obviously a high temperature.' Isandro's glance slid once more to the figure lying on the bed. Her nightdress clung damply to her and the pinpoints of bright red colour stood out livid against the pallor of her skin. 'Nausea…have you been sick?'

Now they decided to acknowledge she was there. 'Mind your own damned business!'

The middle-aged medic laughed and suggested that Mr Montero might like to leave while he had a chat with the patient.

The doctor confirmed that Zoe had a dose of the bug doing the rounds and suggested she take an analgesic for her temperature, get plenty of rest and take lots of fluids.

'Which is what I was doing,' Zoe told Isandro.

'What can I get you?'

'Just go away and leave me alone.'

When the cranky invalid refused point-blank to be nursed or cosseted he did the next best thing—he offered to take the twins off her hands for the rest of the day.

An offer that did not strike him as odd until with the twins in tow he bumped into a school friend of Dana's in a hands-on science exhibition. Emma, who had her youngest in tow, was one of the few mutual friends that he had stayed in contact with after the divorce. Her parting shot of 'I'd really like to meet the woman who has domesticated you!' had stayed with him.

Ridiculous, of course—he hadn't changed in any fundamental way. He could walk away from this relationship at any time. He enjoyed the twins, they amused him…though they were exhausting.

Denial, Isandro, mocked the voice in his head.

The next day Zoe felt tired. Her head ached and things still hurt, but she was well enough to get up, which was just as well as she had promised to go the airport this morning to pick up Chloe, John and Hannah. She also needed to drop the kids off for their science field trip before—oh, God, just thinking about the day ahead made her headache worse.

'Get a wriggle on, you two!' she yelled, pulling open the front door as Harry vanished to find his rucksack he had left 'somewhere.'

'What the hell do you think you are doing?'

Zoe reacted to the angry voice like a bullet zinging past her ear and spun around to face the tall figure who was striding up the path to the front door. He looked dauntingly angry, but Zoe, refusing to be daunted, pressed a hand to her throbbing head and returned belligerently, 'I might ask you the same thing. I thought you had a meeting in Paris today.'

'It was cancelled.' The lie came smoothly. Intercepting the direction of her gaze, he lifted the hand that held a large bouquet of flowers. 'The gardener heard you were unwell.'

It seemed unnecessary to Isandro to explain that he had told him. 'He says you prefer the flowers that have a scent to the hothouse roses…?'

'I do! How lovely of him,' she exclaimed, taking the fragrant ribbon-tied posy and lifting it to her nose. 'I must thank him.'

'I will pass on your message and you will go back to bed.'

Her chin went up at his dictatorial attitude. 'You can't just waltz in here and order me around. I'm fine and I have to pick up Chloe and co from the airport after I've taken the twins to—'

'Bed!' Isandro thundered just as the postman opened the garden gate.

'Nice morning,' the man said as he handed a pink-faced Zoe her letters.

'Well, thank you for that.' Zoe glared up at Isandro.

Georgie's voice cut across her. 'Isandro's here, Harry, he's taking us to school.'

Mortified, Zoe shook her head. The boundaries of their relationship did blur on occasion but she was sure they would not stretch to the school run! 'No, no, he's not… Georgie, go—'

'Yes, I am. Go get in the car,' he said, directing this order to the twins, who ran out before Zoe could say a word.

'You're not!'

'I am.' Ignoring her squeal of furious protest, he snatched the car keys that were dangling from her fingers and put them in the pocket of his well-cut trousers. 'Now be a good girl and go back to bed.'

'Do not treat me like a child.' Even if I sound like one.

He looked impatient. 'You are clearly still unwell. You look terrible.' It was not his job to make her better, so why the hell had he taken it on himself to do so?

She gave a twisted smile. 'Thanks.' He must be right otherwise the comment would not have made her feel like crying.

'If you drag yourself out of bed unnecessarily you will only delay your recovery.'

In a perfect world another twenty-four hours would have been nice. 'So now you're a doctor.'

'You are a very bad patient.'

'I need to—'

'Has it not occurred to you that Chloe and her family will not thank you for infecting them with your flu bug?'

Zoe's face fell. 'I hadn't thought of that.'

Hands on her shoulders, he turned her around. 'So go back to bed, and for once in your life, woman, let someone else be in charge.' He broke off at the sound of a car horn. 'That is my car.'

He was being summoned by a pair of kids, and he was responding!

Zoe tried to remember the last time she had felt in charge and gave a small bitter laugh. 'This from the world's biggest control freak!' she muttered as the door closed.

By the time she reached her bed Zoe was too tired to undress. She fell on top of it fully dressed and fell into a deep sleep.

When she woke, the afternoon sun was shining through the window and she wasn't alone. She raised herself up on one elbow and gazed down at the man lying beside her. He too was fully dressed and sound asleep.

Or maybe not.

Isandro opened his heavy-lidded eyes and stretched a hand above his head; he had not slept the previous night but fortunately he survived well on catnaps.

He looked so gorgeous that it hurt; the pain was physical.

She was trailing her fingers lovingly down his cheek when it hit her. 'Chloe!' she yelped, glancing with horror at the time on the digital display of her alarm. 'I thought you were—'

She bit her lip—an assumption she should not have made. He had taken the twins to school because that had been pretty much a fait accompli, but the last thing Isandro wanted was involvement in her domestic life. He just wanted her in bed…for how long?

She pushed away this depressing thought.

'Relax, I have sent a car for them.' He gave a yawn. He was sure that nursing did not involve falling asleep beside your patient, but the last twenty-four hours had taught Isandro that he was not a natural nurse and when Zoe had thrashed around restlessly and muttered his name in her sleep he had found himself unable not to respond. His physical closeness had seemed to soothe her.

'Their flight arrived on time and they are on their way home.'

'Thank you…I'm really sorry about being a nuisance…'

He reached and placed a hand behind her neck, his fingertips sending little flickers of electricity through her body as they pushed into her hairline.

'You are always a nuisance.' She turned his

ordered life into total chaos and yet still he kept coming back for more…?

Zoe struggled to read his expression. 'The twins can be very—'

'I never do anything I do not want to do, *querida*.'

'You can't want to run the twins around and—'

He dragged her face down to his until their noses were touching. 'Right now I want—'

'Do you always get what you want?' she whispered against his warm lips… God, but he smelt incredible.

'I have that reputation.'

'What was that for?' she asked huskily when the long, languid kiss ended.

'Chloe sent her love.'

'Not like that, she didn't.'

His throaty laugh made her grin.

'You shouldn't be kissing me. I'm probably infectious.'

He stroked her cheek. 'I have an excellent immune system. I never get ill.'

You never get in love. She pushed the thought away. Why spoil what she had by wishing for something she never could have? It was hard sometimes.

'Thanks for this morning.'

He shrugged and levered himself into a sitting position before dragging both hands through his sexily ruffled dark hair.

'You should go. The twins will be home soon.' She swung her legs over the side of the bed, not seeing the flicker of annoyance that moved across his taut lean features. 'I really am feeling better now. I needed that sleep.'

After scanning her face, he nodded and got up from the bed. 'I have arranged for Rowena to pick up the twins after their field trip,' he said, rising with fluid grace to his feet. 'And there is something that Mrs Whittaker called a casserole in the fridge. Apparently all you have to do is heat it up.'

'That's so kind of her.'

'I'm flying to Paris in the morning.'

By the time he turned back at the door Zoe had wiped her face clean of the ludicrous disappointment she had felt at his casual disclosure.

'Oh, and Polly is not expecting you in work until Monday.'

As the door closed she picked up the phone. 'Polly—no, that's why I'm ringing. I'm fine— I'll be in work tomorrow.'

Even if it killed her it was too late not to fall in love with Isandro, but she was damned if she was going to let him micro-manage every aspect of her life. She had to make her own decisions, stay independent. He wasn't going to be around for ever.

CHAPTER TEN

INITIALLY IT HAD BEEN scary working in the gallery, but Zoe had soon gained more confidence and now she loved it. Especially since Polly had begun to give her responsibility, which she thrived on.

Today had been a good one. A buyer for an insurance firm had left having purchased several very expensive pastels by a new up-and-coming artist, and there was a spring in her step when Zoe finally locked up the gallery and fastened her jacket against the cold breeze blowing down the street. She was wondering if she'd make the early train when the loud honk of a car horn made her look up.

Pulled up beside the pavement, showing a selfish disregard for the parking restrictions, was a car she recognised. Her heart picked up tempo as she walked towards it, and as she reached it the window on the driver's side rolled down.

'What are you doing here?'

Isandro smiled. He hadn't actually known where he was heading until he had arrived just as she was emerging from the gallery. The sight of her slim, trim figure had, if not lifted his spirits, definitely alleviated the gloom.

'I'm heading home. Do you want a lift?'

The terse delivery made her look more closely at him, her brow furrowing as she studied his face. There was nothing specific, but she could tell that something was wrong.

'That would be good—my feet are killing me,' she admitted.

They had been driving along in total silence for ten minutes before she spoke. 'So what's wrong?'

He flashed her an impatient sideways glance. 'Nothing is wrong… What makes you think anything is wrong?'

'You haven't said a word.'

'Can't a man enjoy a little silence? Do we have

to indulge in an endless stream of boring, meaningless drivel?'

She let out a long silent whistle. 'If you're going to speak to me in that tone you can drop me off.'

By way of reply he pressed his foot on the accelerator. 'Don't be so bloody touchy.'

'Me! So are you going to tell me what's wrong?' She gripped the door and closed her eyes as they approached a hairpin bend. 'Or are you going to drive us off the road?'

'I am perfectly in control of this car.'

Despite his reply she was relieved that he did perceptively slow his speed as the powerful car came out of the bend.

'I heard from my father today.' He compressed his sensual lips hard enough to rim them with white in a physical effort to stem the flow of information.

'That's nice.' Clearly it wasn't, and prodding gently was a dangerous strategy but she couldn't think of any other way to get him to open up. It was obvious to her he needed to even if he was too pig-headed to admit it.

Was there some problem between him and his father...? He had mentioned his mother once in past tense, and as he'd never said anything about his father she had always assumed that both his parents were dead.

'Nice!' he snarled.

Zoe's confusion and concern grew as her gaze travelled from his white-knuckled hands on the wheel to his taut profile.

'Sorry, is it bad news?' He couldn't accuse her of prying when he had introduced the subject... not that he wouldn't if it suited him, she thought with a wry smile.

'He's invited me to his wedding.' He elaborated, but as the additional information was in his native Spanish she was none the wiser.

'I suppose it's hard to see your father moving on. Has your mother been dead long?' Her blue eyes shone with sympathy as she looked at him through her lashes.

'Moving on!' His teeth came together with an audible grating sound. 'You think this is my problem?'

'It's only natural, especially if you were close to your mother—'

'My father moved on so fast the headstone was still being carved. My father—' He broke off, a nerve in his taut jaw clenching as he stared with white-faced intensity at the road ahead.

'There's a layby up ahead. Pull over, Isandro,' she said quietly.

'Why?'

She had wondered why he had chosen the minor road, a slightly longer route, in preference to the shorter journey on the motorway. Now she was glad; at least this road was almost empty.

'Because I don't particularly want to end up a road-traffic-accident statistic.' For a moment she thought he was going to ignore her, but to her intense relief at the last moment he swerved into the layby, sending up a shower of gravel.

He turned off the engine, and without a word got out of the car. Leaving the door wide open, he began to pace up and down on the grassy verge of the road.

Zoe didn't follow him. Isandro was a man who

needed space, so she let him walk while he fought the devils that drove him. He couldn't not be elegant—the animal grace was an integral part of him, and even vibrating with anger he was riveting to watch.

This was a part of his personality he concealed behind a carefully contrived mask. This was the part of his personality that he liked to deny— the passion and fire—allowing it out only behind closed doors. She knew from experience that driving something underground didn't make it go away; it just consumed you.

Ignoring the fact she had fallen in love with him had not lessened her feelings. It had just meant that when it surfaced… She shivered and wrapped her arms protectively around herself, hugging tight. She wouldn't let it surface.

She stayed silent when he finally slid back into the car.

'What do you think?'

'About what, Isandro?'

'I was twenty-one when my mother died, and already married.'

Zoe had lost her own father when she was a baby and she had no memory of him. Her mother's death remained a strong and sad memory, even though at the end it had been a release.

'My father was a wreck. Then two months after she died, out of the blue he rang and told me he'd met a wonderful woman who reminded him of my mother.' His lips curled into a contemptuous smile. 'Turned out the wonderful woman had a sweet daughter who he planned to adopt. And yes, the likeness to my mother was startling. It became obvious pretty quickly to everyone but him that she was a con artist. Friends, colleagues told him...'

'You told him?'

Isandro nodded. 'He told me I was jealous. When they finally did a flit, he was one step away from bankruptcy. He'd mortgaged my mother's home, sold off her jewellery, and...' His chest heaved as he struggled to contain his feelings.

'And now he's met someone else?'

'Apparently.'

'And he's invited you to the wedding?'

She got another nod.

'Do you really want to know what I think?'

'I asked, didn't I?' The belated realisation sent a wave of shock through his body. One of the reasons Dana had cited for the breakdown of their marriage was the fact that, according to her, he never listened to her, or asked her opinion.

I need to be needed, Isandro, and you don't need me—you don't need anyone.

He had not disputed it, because it had been true… It still was.

Zoe arched a delicate brow and wondered about the odd expression on his face. 'That doesn't mean you won't yell if I say something you don't want to hear.'

He pushed his dark head back into the leather headrest and gave a half-smile as he looked at her from under the dark mesh of his preposterously long eyelashes.

'Since when has that stopped you?'

Zoe was the only woman who ever challenged him. She didn't go out of her way to say what he wanted to hear, and sometimes it seemed to him she took a perverse pleasure from winding him up.

'I think you should go to the wedding and wish your father well.'

He clenched his jaw and swore under his breath.

Zoe didn't let his response throw her. It was pretty much what she had anticipated. 'Well, not going isn't going to stop him. I know he screwed up once, but who doesn't?'

'He didn't just screw up, he—'

'He thought he was in love. That's not a crime.' Though Isandro's expression suggested he thought it should be. 'I'm sure he feels pretty stupid about what happened. Ashamed and embarrassed.'

'I suppose so.' Isandro rubbed his jaw. Had he ever really thought about how his father felt? Would a stronger man have shown more compassion?

He turned his brooding gaze on Zoe. Such uncomfortable thoughts had never come to him before.

'And I expect he knows you're still angry with him.'

'I'm not…' He caught her eyes once more and sighed, dragging a hand through his sable hair until it stood up in tufts around his bronzed face.

'All right, I am angry… How could he take the word of that woman and not his friends, people who he had known for years?'

'You, you mean?'

He shrugged and issued his response through clenched teeth. 'It is not important.'

Zoe felt her heart squeeze in her chest in sympathy. 'It must have been hurtful.'

Isandro looked from the blue eyes brimming with sympathy to the hand that lay on his arm and thought, What the hell am I doing?

Regretting the outburst that had made him reveal so much of his feelings, and equating it with weakness, he slid his arm from under her hand. He was not a man who shared his problems. His cure for extreme frustration was mind-numbing laps of the pool, or a run that battered body and mind into numbness.

This time he had not sought the pool or donned

his running shoes. He had… Why had instinct made him seek out Zoe?

'What was hurtful, as you put it,' he countered in a harsh voice, 'was being forced to put my own life on hold and pull in every favour I had owing in order to stop the firm going under and my father ending up in jail. It wasn't just his money the bitch got. He'd "borrowed" from clients' accounts.'

Zoe watched the shutters go back up, hearing the lack of emotion in his hard voice. She could have screamed in sheer frustration, but instead she put her hand back in her lap, her feelings seesawing violently between empathy and a strong desire to shake him.

Did he imagine allowing her even a glimpse of the man beneath the mask gave her some sort of special power?

'Don't worry, Isandro, I'd already guessed you're actually human.' Their glances connected and Zoe saw the shock he was not quick enough to hide flicker in the second before his hooded eyelids lowered, leaving her looking at the gleam of his eyes through the mesh of his eyelashes. 'But I won't tell anyone. Your secret is safe with me,' she promised.

His lips tightened, but the faint flush along the angle of his cheekbones suggested she had made her point. 'I am not in the mood for word games, Zoe.'

'Fine, is this straightforward enough? Your dad made a mistake once…all right, a big mistake,' she conceded in response to his snort. 'That doesn't mean there isn't an outside possibility he actually loves this woman.'

His lip curled contemptuously. 'My father believes in fairy tales.' While he despised the childlike credulity, there had been moments when Isandro almost envied his father.

'Isn't that a good thing? That the awful woman didn't win?' she said softly.

The suggestion caused Isandro to turn his head sharply to look at her, the compassion glowing in her eyes as much as the statement causing him to frown. A nerve jumped spasmodically in his lean cheek. A man was allowed some privacy, yet she continually ignored the 'keep off' signs and crossed the boundaries.

Didn't you invite her in when you offloaded your emotional garbage?

His frown deepened as he pushed away the question and barked, 'How do you figure that one out?'

Watching as she stuck out her chin to a belligerent angle, he felt his anger slipping away to be replaced with an emotion he was less comfortable putting a name to. The woman had more guts than anyone he had ever met.

'If your father had come out of the experience a cynic she would have won, but he hasn't. He hasn't become bitter, cynical and twisted.'

She saw the flicker of an emotion she could not name in his dark eyes before he turned his head away from her. The rain had begun to drum against the window.

'Are you saying I have?'

Instead of responding to the question, she voiced one that had popped into her head during the conversation. 'Is that why your marriage failed?'

He turned to face her and instead, as she half expected, of telling her to mind her own business, shook his head and repeated the question.

'Is what why my marriage failed?'

Did he lay the blame for his failed marriage at his father's door? It would certainly go a long way to explain why, all these years later, he could not forgive and forget. Common sense told her this was a subject she shouldn't broach but a need to understand this man who had captured her heart was stronger. 'You were forced to concentrate your energy on saving your father and the firm and you didn't have time for your...' Her voice faltered as she stopped and gave a self-conscious shrug. 'It's none of my business. I just...'

'Want to pry and prod.'

Encouraged that he sounded amused, but not antagonistic, she lifted her gaze, studying his face as he replied.

'No, my marriage did not fail because I was busy rebuilding the company. Though I imagine it might have speeded up the process. Simply put, my marriage was never my priority. We married too young—we both wanted different things from life. Marriage requires compromise.' His dark eyes brushed her face. 'I do not do compromise.' He gave a sardonic smile, to which she had no response. 'The end was inevitable.'

Did this clinical analysis hide a broken heart Isandro could not admit to even to himself?

'I was not surprised when Dana left.' One side of his mobile mouth lifted in an ironic half-smile. 'Though I was not expecting her to leave with my best friend,' he conceded.

Unable to control her reaction, Zoe gasped.

Isandro placed a finger under her chin and lifted it. 'The open-mouth look is not so bad on you.' Head tilted a little to one side, he drew back slightly to look at her face, realising as he did so that nothing was a bad look on her.

His eyes darkened as he ran the pad of his thumb down her smooth, downy soft cheek. Inhaling the scent of her warm skin through flared nostrils, he felt the desire that was always close to the surface. Unable to resist the lush softness of her mouth, he bent his head, feeling her sigh as she opened her mouth to deepen the penetration of his tongue, winding her fingers into his hair, pulling him in close.

When he lifted his mouth they stayed that way, her nose pressed to the side of his, her fingers in his hair, their warm breaths mingling.

Reluctant to break physical contact, she slid her hands slowly down over his broad muscular shoulders before crossing them across her stomach in a protective hug. She was still shaking in response to the soul-stripping kiss, the barely leashed violence in his embrace; the simmering hunger still in his eyes made it hard for her to speak, let alone focus.

She felt his hand go to her breasts, cupping them through her clothes, as his other hand skimmed down the side of her face.

She was breathing hard now; her fingers went to his belt.

'If anyone comes…' she said thickly.

He pulled down his jeans and reached across

to slide her skirt up her thighs, his fingers sliding up her silky warm skin under the hem of her
panties.

'They won't.'

His hard, predatory expression made her shiver
inside. Excited and aroused beyond reason or
caution, she climbed onto his lap, facing him.
His hands moved in a sweeping motion up and
down her back and down her buttocks before
coming to rest on her hips.

He wanted her so badly that he couldn't breathe;
all he could think about was sinking into her. It
was crazy and intense.

Zoe reached down to caress his shaft, waiting
until he was groaning before she raised herself
up and impaled herself on the hard, silky, hot
length. Perfectly in tune, they moved together
fast and hard in perfect harmony until they both
came in a hot, violent flood.

Adjusting her clothes, aware that beside her
Isandro was doing the same, she could hardly believe what she had just done. Anyone could have
driven by and seen them, and she hadn't cared.

Her body still warm with the flush of desire, she turned to look at him.

'I'm sorry. I didn't know about… It must have been terrible for you.' Dana was a beautiful name. Had she been beautiful? Of course she'd been beautiful.

And he'd loved her… Zoe was shocked by the animosity she felt towards a woman she had never met. Had he been thinking about her while he made love just now?

It took him a few seconds to realise what she was talking about—his ex-wife! They had just made devastating love and she was talking about his ex. He didn't want to talk about Dana; he wanted to talk about where this was going. He wanted to talk about having Zoe in his bed nights.

'I was a hell of a husband. Basically I lived my own life and expected her to take it or leave it. In the end, she left it. I do not blame her. She was lonely and Carl was able to give her the things she wanted.' He held her blue eyes as he said, 'Some men are not meant for marriage.'

The warning was implicit. Wondering uneasily what she'd done to make him feel the need to spell out the obvious, she pulled her hands out from the warmth of his and laughed.

'I suppose there's still time to cancel the engagement notice I sent to the paper. Relax, Isandro, I'm not about to propose.'

And not even in her wildest dreams had she ever imagined Isandro doing so. She had accepted that what they had would never be deep and meaningful for him. What choice did she have? She was taking it one day at a time, enjoying the moments when they were together. Perhaps the knowledge that they would not last gave them a sweet bitterness, but she was determined not to waste a second.

Isandro leaned back in his own seat and turned his head to look at her. 'So you think I should go to my father's wedding?'

'Does it matter what I think?'

'Sometimes an objective view is good.'

Zoe laughed, the sound dredged from somewhere deep inside her bubbling from her lips. She couldn't help herself—objective where Isandro was concerned was something she could never be.

Biting her lip to stem the flow, she responded to his quizzical look with a shrug. 'I thought I was emotional and illogical?'

'You have the occasional lucid moment,' he threw back with a lazy grin.

'So will you go?'

'There is no point in burning my bridges.'

Zoe nodded and lowered her gaze. She had burnt her bridges some time ago. Would she regret it…? She shook her head; she didn't want to think about that now.

She glanced at her watch and was shocked to see how long they had been here. 'I need to pick up the twins. I promised Chloe's mum-in-law I'd pick them up at half past.' It was almost that time now. While she was being utterly selfish she would never let her own selfish desires come ahead of her duty to her sister's children.

'Calm down—it won't take long.'

It didn't. He delivered her to the cottage door only five minutes late. Zoe got out of the car.

About to join her, Isandro paused and responded to the bleep of his mobile.

He scanned the screen and with a curse slid it back into his pocket. 'Are you all right getting home alone?'

'Of course.'

'I will see you…' He paused, as if unable to commit himself even to a minor thing like a time, and, nodding curtly, slammed the door and drove off.

CHAPTER ELEVEN

STRUGGLING TO PUSH all thoughts of Isandro from her head, Zoe tapped on the cottage door and walked inside the warm, homely, farmhouse-style kitchen. A second later the impossible was achieved: she wasn't thinking of Isandro.

'Oh, my God!' She dropped to her knees in front of the child seated at the table, her face creased in lines of anxiety as she touched the uninjured side of her nephew's face. 'Harry!'

'It's fine.'

Maud was on her feet, laying a hand on Zoe's shoulder.

'Seriously, it's a lot worse than it looks, dear.'

'How on earth...? Who did this? Has a doctor seen...?'

'The nurse at school cleaned the cut.' Georgie, who had come to stand beside her brother, provided the information to a stunned Zoe.

'But who did this to you, Harry? Why didn't the headmaster inform me?'

'Sit down, dear, you've had a shock.' Maud pushed Zoe down into a chair beside Harry and produced a cup of tea from somewhere. 'The head tried to ring you but you'd already left and your mobile was switched off.'

'He wants to see you tomorrow,' Harry muttered, licking his bruised and swollen lip.

'And I want to see him! I want to know the little thug who—your poor face…'

'It wasn't Adam, it was Harry. He just went for him.'

Zoe turned her head to look at Georgie. 'Harry fighting…?' She shook her head. The image of gentle, sweet Harry brawling was one she simply couldn't accept. Now, if it had been Georgie…

'He was. I saw it.'

'But, Harry, why?'

The little boy shook his head and looked away. It was Georgie who responded.

'It was the things Adam was saying about you and Isandro. I was telling him he was stupid but

Harry came in just when Adam called you a bad name and Harry went for him… He was brilliant,' she enthused, turning an admiring look at her twin.

Digesting the information in shock, Zoe recovered enough to knock this on the head. 'It is never brilliant to fight,' she said numbly.

Oh, God, this was her fault!

Of this Zoe had no doubt. The child in question was the son of the attractive vet who had made a play for Isandro at Chloe's party. The woman had gone out of her way ever since to be unpleasant to Zoe, and she had no doubt the kid was only repeating what he had heard at home. Probably everyone was saying the same with various degrees of contempt.

How could she not have considered the possible fallout for the twins when she had embarked on this affair? She had thought that by keeping the affair from them she was protecting them… Some protection, she thought, self-disgust bubbling like acid in her stomach.

She patted Harry's curly head. 'Don't worry, I'll make things right with the headmaster.'

'I told you not to tell, Georgie. Look, she's crying now.'

Zoe gave a watery smile and sniffed. 'No, I'm not crying. And I'm very, very cross with you.'

The kiss she then planted on Harry's head might have given mixed messages, but what mattered was putting this right. And she would. The sooner, the better. No gingerly easing off the plaster—it was a straight in there, hold your breath, grit your teeth and rip it off. The brutal approach might sting a bit at the time but why prolong the agony?

So the analogy was not perfect. No matter what spin she put on it, Zoe knew that this was going to hurt more than losing a few superficial layers of epidermis, but the important thing was not giving herself time for her resolve to weaken and waver.

That had been the theory anyway. But it was after eleven when the doorbell finally rang and by this time Zoe had gone through nail-biting apprehension and nervous pacing and come out the other side.

She let the doorbell ring a second time before she took a deep breath and headed for the hall. I'm totally calm, she told herself, serene even.

Her serenity lasted all the way up to the door and it swung inwards to reveal a tall, lean figure looking sleek and exclusive in a designer suit and, frankly, well out of her league. It hadn't been intended to last... They were a total mismatch outside the bedroom. She took a deep breath and pushed away thoughts of the bedroom and reminded herself all she was doing was hastening the inevitable.

So suck it up, Zoe, you're a grown-up, a parent...running away or, even worse, running into his arms is not an option.

'Sorry I'm so late...' Drawn irresistibly to her body heat and softness, he began to lean forward, but was forced to draw back when she whisked away and began to walk towards the sitting room. His expression thoughtful, he watched her retreating back. It grew less thoughtful as his heavy-lidded eyes lingered on her rounded bottom. He shook his head to clear it. 'I hope the food isn't spoilt.'

'I didn't make any food.' Her spine stiff with tension, she walked ahead of him into the sitting room, trying desperately to remember her carefully prepared speech. It had vanished into the ether, or at least into some dark dead end of her stressed brain.

He had caught the negative vibes even before she avoided his embrace. Isandro's expression grew contemptuous as he asked himself what point exactly he had been making when he hadn't rung to say he'd be late.

It was simply another example of his increasingly pathetic attempts to pretend that this was all casual. Who was he kidding anyway?

Well, there, he'd admitted it, but this wasn't the time to rush on and make any dramatic declarations. Clearly if he wanted to keep Zoe in his bed and in his life he would have to bend some of his normal rules.

The painful acknowledgement had an aftertaste of relief to it… He felt a little of the tension in his shoulders release. Why on earth had that been so difficult? It wasn't as if he hadn't been bending the bloody rules to breaking point from the moment her blue eyes, sinuous curves and smart mouth appeared in his world.

Life was about to change, and he wasn't infatuated; he was…past infatuation.

Still unwilling to follow this insight through to its conclusion, he closed the door of the sitting room behind him. He should be opening doors. The contemplative furrow in his brow smoothed.

It was not a weakness to accept he wanted more from this relationship than sex, it was a weakness not to accept it.

He clapped a hand to his head. Will you listen to yourself, Isandro? the analytical portion of his brain mocked. This was exactly the reason he didn't go in for all that self-analysis crap. It could drive a man crazy and get him nowhere, especially when he'd not had a full night's sleep for how long…?

Before, he had never spent a full night with a

woman out of his own choice. But now the roles were reversed and, back in his own bed, for some reason he just lay awake unable to sleep without her warmth in his arms.

Boyfriend… He tried the description on for size in his head. He'd never actually been anyone's boyfriend. The whole idea seemed…not him.

Her initial impression of intense weariness was more pronounced when he walked into the small living room. It was palpable. It took every ounce of her self-control to fight the compelling urge to rush to him.

He paused, appearing to sense her mood before he tilted his head towards the ceiling and said in a hushed voice, 'The children?'

'Are asleep.'

He expelled a sigh, silenced the narrative in his head and extended his arms. It did not cross his mind for one moment that she would not run into them. Zoe was more responsive to him than any other woman he had ever met. If his passion for her was unquenchable, so was hers for him.

She was infatuated.

She's in love.

Zoe stood, her feet glued to the spot, and shook her head. The effort caused beads of sweat to form on her upper lip, but she dabbed them with her tongue and shook her head.

He did not approach her, but instead closed the door behind him and leaned his broad shoulders against the wall. He looked very pale. His dark eyes were weirdly blank, they reminded her of someone in shock.

He cleared his throat. 'Problem?'

She laughed even though she felt like crying. That was so like Isandro, who never used two words when one would suffice. Then, gathering her determination in both hands, she nodded.

'This isn't working.'

He would appreciate brevity, she decided, stifling an irrational stab of guilt. It wasn't as if Isandro had invested any emotions in this relationship. It would be a mistake to imagine that he would feel as though he'd lost a limb if she vanished from his life.

The highly charged silence stretched and pulsed, then he laughed and broke the spell.

She cleared her throat. Either he was more all right with this than she had imagined or he was not taking her seriously. 'I'm not joking. I think we should agree to call it a day.'

He stopped laughing. 'You do?'

She nodded, then cleared her throat. She had seen granite walls more revealing than his expression. The only things moving were the muscles in his brown throat as they rippled under the surface of his bronzed skin. 'Yes.'

Isandro closed his eyes, fighting the urge to yell. The children were upstairs sleeping and he could not yell; he had to appear invisible.

Her insistence on maintaining the unrealistic illusion they were nothing but passing acquaintances had not seemed a big ask at the time. It had even seemed like a good idea. However, it had ceased to feel like a good idea some time ago.

There was a certain dark irony to the situation. He had always avoided having his name linked with a woman, and now he was with a woman who seemed ashamed to acknowledge they were sleeping together.

It should have been the ideal situation, but it wasn't.

The previous week he had driven past the school when she was picking up the twins. They had waved and Zoe had pretended not to see him. He had been contemplating leaping out of the car and hauling her into his arms and kissing her in front of the entire damned gossipy village whose opinion seemed to matter so much to her. It wasn't as if they didn't all know they were sleeping together anyway.

But he hadn't, because he wasn't a Neanderthal. Though lately he had seen there were certain advantages in following your baser instincts.

Obviously he did not want to set up house, but neither did he want to be treated like a dirty secret... It was demeaning for any man.

'You need a drink.'

Zoe felt panic as she watched him shrug off his jacket before walking across to the cupboard where she had put the half-drunk bottle of wine he had opened the previous evening.

'I don't drink, remember?' She took a deep breath, lowered her voice from the shrill, unattractive level it had risen to and reminded him, 'We agreed that when this didn't work we would simply call it a day. Look, I know it must be strange because you assumed—actually so did I—that it would be you who ended things.' She gave a sad smile. 'It's nothing personal,' she added earnestly.

He studied her face for any sign of irony but there was none. 'Well, I do want a drink,' he said, pouring the remnants of the bottle into a glass and swallowing the contents without tasting.

'So nothing personal, which of course makes all the difference,' he drawled, setting aside the glass with elaborate care while in his head he saw it smashing to a million pieces as he threw it into the fireplace.

'Please don't be like that,' she begged. 'This is hard.' She bit her trembling lip. She could not afford to lose her focus now, she could not afford to allow him to touch her...

'This is bloody ridiculous,' he contended, thrusting his balled fists into the pockets of his well-cut trousers and glaring at her.

Zoe recognised the cause of his belligerence but she was not in the mood to show much understanding for injured male pride. So maybe he had just been dumped for the first time in his life. There were any number of nubile women who would be gagging to massage his ego.

She, on the other hand, might never fall in love again. This man was her soulmate, and all he could do was sulk while her heart was damned well breaking.

Well, at least he should remember her, though for all the wrong reasons—as the woman who dared to dump him!

'I know you said we could stay on here,' she said formally, 'but that wouldn't be right. I have made alternative arrangements.'

'You have what?' he roared as his smouldering

temper sparked into full-blown conflagration. 'Since when is this not working?'

She kept her chin up, not easy when a man who appeared to be ten feet tall was towering over her like some sort of damned volcano. 'Since Harry came home with a black eye and a split lip after brawling with a boy who called me a cheap tart, among other things.'

Isandro took a step back, the air leaving his lungs in one audible, sizzling hiss.

CHAPTER TWELVE

'IS HE ALL RIGHT?'

Mingled with the protective outrage Isandro felt was a surge of pride that the boy had stood up for his aunt; he had protected her honour.

Which was more than he had done. The guilty knowledge that this situation was one of his making scratched away at Isandro's conscience like a nail on a blackboard.

No complications? He had known that was a total impossibility from day one. He had tried extremely hard to tell himself otherwise but he had known that this thing could get very complicated. He had taken refuge in technicalities—Zoe no longer worked for him; he never spent the entire night. He should have seen this coming. But he had wanted her…needed her with a hunger that was totally outside his experience. And in order to satisfy that hunger he had been prepared to break any and all rules.

She nodded, the concern now in his dark eyes making her tear up. 'He will be.'

She rubbed a stray tear with the back of her hand, and the gesture made Isandro's throat tighten.

'This is a small village and people gossip. It was unrealistic of me not to expect this, and selfish of me not to consider the effect this sort of affair would have on the twins.'

'So you think that nobody in this village has sex outside marriage?'

The sarcasm in his voice brought a flush to her pale cheeks. 'That's not the point.'

'What are you going to do—take a vow of chastity until the twins leave home? No boyfriends? That is your idea of preparing them for the real world?'

'You're not my boyfriend. We don't have a relationship—we have sex.'

'Or do you need a ring on your finger? Is that what this is about?'

'Of course not. It's not sex outside marriage, it's sex with you!' she yelled before she remembered the sleeping children.

He did not respond to her announcement at all, though his feet-apart stance and stony, tight-lipped silence did not exactly convey happiness.

'I don't want to argue.' She gave a weary sigh and looked at him through her lashes, head tilted a little to one side. Seeing the familiar attitude, he felt his anger levels decrease.

'But it's true—you're not my boyfriend. And I didn't mean it to sound the way it did about sex with you, but it is true as well... How can I tell the children that sex within a loving, caring relationship can be a beautiful thing, when I'm having sex with you?' While it might be beautiful for her, she knew that for Isandro it was simply an act of physical release.

If ever she had come close to reading more into his exquisite tenderness and mind-blowing passion, she reminded herself of this: it was just sex for Isandro, for all that he did 'just sex' very well indeed.

He arched a sardonic brow. 'So you are only sleeping with me to pay for the rent.'

The suggestion brought a rosy tinge of anger to her pale cheeks. How dared he act like the injured party?

'Of course I'm not! I'd sleep with you if I had to crawl across a desert to get into your bed.' Her blue eyes held his, shining with passionate fervour, before she dropped her gaze, remembering a few crucial seconds late that she was ending a relationship, not declaring he was her drug of choice...legal but, oh, so addictive.

'But this isn't about what I want.' She inhaled and struggled to clear the haze of desire in her brain. The memory of Harry's bruised little face did the trick better than a bucket of cold water. She squared her slender shoulders and lifted her chin. 'It's what I need to do for the twins. I have to send out the right message and I know full well that even—'

His eyes held a complacent gleam as he added helpfully, 'You would crawl across a desert to sleep with me?'

As if he didn't already know that! Zoe slung him a cross look and sniffed. He wasn't making this any easier.

'A figure of speech,' she muttered, knowing it had been much more than that and hoping he didn't. 'We're really not discussing how great you are in bed.'

'Sex with you is worth the odd desert crossing, too.'

Even above the presence of his painful arousal, Isandro was conscious of a strange heaviness in his chest as he made a conscious effort to capture Zoe's eyes. She seemed determined to look anywhere but at him. The moment of success when he welded his sloe-black eyes on her bright burning blue… The heaviness in his chest bordered unbearable… Yet he felt strangely exhilarated. Was he having a heart attack?

Zoe licked her dry lips and struggled to think past the static buzz of electricity in the room.

'Thanks…' she said, not knowing what else to say, and not hearing the huskiness in her voice above the deafening clamour of her pounding pulses. 'Children can be very cruel.' She gave a loud sniff. 'So you see that I can't continue to live here to be your…mistress.'

'You are not my mistress.'

His offended hauteur in his attitude struck her as weird. 'I live here, and you own the place.'

'You pay rent.'

'A token amount. And the fact is you wouldn't have offered me this place if we hadn't been having sex.'

'I have never paid for sex.'

'We can play table tennis semantics all night, but it won't stop other people seeing me as a kept woman.'

'I don't give a damn what people think.'

'That's not a luxury I can afford, Isandro,' she said sadly. 'It stopped being the day I took on the twins. It's my job to be a good role model for them. Even if they didn't have to contend with the sort of teasing that happened today, what sort message am I sending?'

'Parents do have sex. That is the reality, and

you cannot protect them from every hurt along the way. I will have a word with the headmaster.'

She stared at him. 'I can't believe you just said that!' she yelped, dropping into a chair.

'Neither can I,' he admitted honestly.

'You will not have any words with the headmaster. You will not go near the school… I want the children to know about adult relationships, know that sex should happen within the confines of a loving relationship. Not like…I may have…' Her eyes filled as she trawled her vocabulary for a word that would cover what she had.

'You're overreacting,' he accused.

She thought of Harry's face and shook her head. 'No,' she said. 'I'm not.'

'You want the children to go to school here. Where will you live? I know Polly well enough to know she's probably paying you a pittance.' Polly would have squeezed a stone dry if it put up her profit margins, and Zoe was too self-deprecating to know her own value.

'I'm learning. She's paying me a fair wage and I've already been looking for suitable accom—'

'Looking!' He pounced on the word like a circling tiger looking for a weakness. 'So this thing with the twins is just an excuse? It's not spontaneous. You were already planning—'

She bit her lip. 'I wasn't planning—preparing.'

Sally at the shop had some holiday lets by the canal—a row of terraced cottages that were empty now the season was over. She was willing to let Zoe have one until she sorted herself something more permanent.

'You can't. I won't let you.'

'You can't stop me. It's my choice.'

'And you think it will be so easy, do you, to spend your nights alone in your solitary single bed?'

She reacted to this deliberate cruelty with a display of stubborn defiance. 'The cottage runs to a double. And who says I'll be alone?'

He was out of his chair and beside her, hauling her to her feet, before she had even finished speaking. His warm breath brushed her cheek as he bent in close. 'Have you been preparing for that, too? Have you met someone?'

She closed her eyes, feeling faint, smelling the citrusy scent of the soap he used. Every instinct she possessed was telling her to sink into all his male hardness, but Zoe fought and from somewhere dredged up the strength to put her hands against his chest and push away.

'I thought your speciality was painless breakups,' she panted as she drew her hair back from her face with a shaky hand. 'Or is that only when you're dictating the timing?'

He didn't respond to the accusation. He was watching her rub her arm where he caught hold of her. He swore and touched her hand lightly; her fingers immediately curled around his. 'Let me see…?'

Zoe shook her head and didn't let go of his finger. The thought of letting go permanently left a great aching hole in her chest.

Would it ever go away?

'It's nothing.'

'The thought of you with another man makes me…' Their eyes connected.

'How could you think there's another man, Isandro?'

'I didn't…I don't. I'm just…' He stopped, let go of her hand and raked his fingers through his hair. 'You can't go, Zoe.'

'Why can't I go?'

'I need you…I love you.' He blinked and looked like a man waking up from a dream. '*Dios*, of course I do. I love you!' he yelled.

She hitched a startled breath and stared up at him. 'Is this your idea of a joke?' she asked him shakily.

'Anything but, *querida*,' he retorted throatily.

'Are you saying this to get me into bed?'

His head reared back as though she had struck him. 'I suppose I deserve that for being so bloody stupid,' he admitted quietly. 'I have been a fool. I was so busy not being a loser like my father that I almost became a loser like me…the biggest loser in the world if I let you walk away from me.'

'You love me?' It still didn't seem real.

'Is that so hard to believe? I can barely stand to have you out of my sight for two seconds. The thought of losing you sent me into a blind panic. I just couldn't admit it, couldn't admit that my fate was no longer in my hands, but that I had put it in yours.' It had taken the prospect of losing her to make him wake up to himself and see what he strongly suspected everyone else already had.

Everyone but Zoe.

He captured her small hands and lifted them to his lips, looking deep into her eyes with an expression that brought tears of joy to them.

'I love you, Isandro.'

'I sort of guessed that.'

She gave a laugh. 'And I thought I was being so subtle.' He pulled her to him and kissed her, a hard, passionate kiss full of promise and love.

'Say it again, Isandro?' she begged huskily.

'I love you, *querida*.' The words that he had been afraid of now came easily; the problem now might be not saying them every second of the day.

'Shall we get married at the hall? Or would you prefer—?'

She drew back her eyes wide. 'Married?'

'Well, how else can I face this headmaster and sort things out for Harry? A boyfriend is not going to have the same pull as a fiancé.'

She blinked, unable to believe this was commitment-phobic Isandro talking. 'You'd do that? Take on the twins?'

'I think the question is more whether they will take me on.'

'Oh, I think they might be OK with it.'

'And you, my love—are you OK with it?'

She smiled and flew into his arms. 'So OK with it, Isandro, so very OK.'

Two months later they attended the wedding of Isandro's father, Raul, in Seville.

It was a lovely wedding, though not, to Zoe's way of thinking, a patch on her own the previous month.

It really pleased her to see Isandro and his father on such good terms. Their little family was growing and soon it would be even bigger.

She had kept the secret to herself two whole days and as the organist struck up the 'Wedding

March' she could hold it in no longer. She leaned across and whispered in Isandro's ear.

He frowned at her and mouthed, 'What?'

She whispered again with the same result. Rolling her eyes, she leaned in and yelled, 'I'm pregnant!'

Of course, it coincided with the music stopping and her announcement echoed off the rafters of the church.

'Why do these things keep happening to me? What is wrong with my timing?'

Isandro, his eyes gleaming, bent towards her. 'Your timing is perfect and as far as I'm concerned you can shout it from the rafters every day... I want the world to know I'm the luckiest man alive.'

Zoe, who had never cried at a wedding before, cried at the second one in two months...tears of pure joy.

* * * * *